修訂三版　108 課綱適用

Cloze Test

克漏字與文意選填

劉美皇 編著

三民書局

國家圖書館出版品預行編目資料

Cloze Test─克漏字與文意選填／劉美皇編著.－－修
訂三版三刷.－－臺北市：三民，2022
面；　公分.－－(英語Make Me High系列)

ISBN 978-957-14-6971-3　(平裝)
1. 英語 2. 問題集

805.189　　　　　　　　　　　　　109015521

Cloze Test
──克漏字與文意選填

編 著 者	劉美皇
發 行 人	劉振強
出 版 者	三民書局股份有限公司
地　　址	臺北市復興北路 386 號 (復北門市) 臺北市重慶南路一段 61 號 (重南門市)
電　　話	(02)25006600
網　　址	三民網路書店 https://www.sanmin.com.tw
出版日期	初版一刷 2003 年 5 月 修訂三版一刷 2020 年 12 月 修訂三版三刷 2022 年 10 月
書籍編號	S804400
I S B N	978-957-14-6971-3

三民書局

序

英語 Make Me High 系列的理想在於超越，在於創新。

這是時代的精神，也是我們出版的動力；

這是教育的目的，也是我們進步的執著。

針對英語的全球化與未來的升學趨勢，

我們設計了一系列適合普高、技高學生的英語學習書籍。

面對英語，不會徬徨不再迷惘，學習的心徹底沸騰，

心情好 High！

實戰模擬，掌握先機知己知彼，百戰不殆決勝未來，

分數更 High！

選擇優質的英語學習書籍，才能激發學習的強烈動機；

興趣盎然便不會畏懼艱難，自信心要自己大聲說出來。

本書如良師指引循循善誘，如益友相互鼓勵攜手成長。

展書輕閱，你將發現……

學習英語原來也可以這麼 High！

Table of Contents

文意選填

COPYRIGHTS AND ACKNOWLEDGEMENTS

"Food Personalities," from INTERACTIONS ONE, a Reading Skills Book, 2nd ed., by Elaine Kirn, © 1990 by McGraw-Hill Companies. Reprinted by permission of the publisher.

"Lie Detectors," from VOANEWS. COM, by Nancy Steinbach, Paul Thompson and Jerilyn Watson.

"Androcles," from INSIDE OUT, Advanced, by Ceri Jones & Tania Bastow, © 2001. Used with kind permission of Macmillan Education, Oxford.

"Netiquette—Internet Dos and Don'ts," from GLOBAL READING BOOK 2, Text, 1st ed., by Neil J. Anderson, © 2003 by Heinle & Heinle, a division of Thomson Learning, Inc. Reprinted by permission of the publisher.

"Understanding United States and Canadian Attitudes Toward Work," from CLUES TO CULTURE: a Cross-Cultural Reading/Writing Book, by Pamela Hartmann, © 1989 by McGraw-Hill Companies. Reprinted by permission of the publisher.

"At Home in a Cave," from EXPRESSIONS 3: Meaningful English Communication, 1st ed., by Nunan, © 2001 by Heinle & Heinle, a division of Thomson Learning, Inc. Reprinted by permission of the publisher.

"Lottery Winner—Rich, but Happy?," from GLOBAL READING BOOK 3, Text, 1st ed., by Neil J. Anderson, © 2003 by Heinle & Heinle, a division of Thomson Learning, Inc. Reprinted by permission of the publisher.

"On the Road: Travel Lifestyles," from INTERACTIONS TWO, a Reading Skills Book, 3rd ed., by Elaine Kirn and Pamela Hartmann, © 1996 by McGraw-Hill Companies. Reprinted by permission of the publisher.

"New Zealand," from GLOBAL VILLAGE ENGLISH, by Matthew McGinniss.

"The Call of the East," from SINORAMA MAGAZINE, July 2002. Reprinted by permission of Sinorama Magazine.

"Formal Letter Writing: A Dying Art?," from GLOBAL READING BOOK 2, Text, 1st ed., by Neil J. Anderson, © 2003 by Heinle & Heinle, a division of Thomson Learning, Inc. Reprinted by permission of the publisher.

"Salmon," from ESSENTIAL READING SKILLS, 1st ed., by John W. Presley & William M. Dodd, © 1982 by Heinle & Heinle, a division of Thomson Learning, Inc. Reprinted by permission of the publisher.

"Human Endurance—What the Body Can Survive," from GLOBAL READING BOOK 2, Text, 1st ed., by Neil J. Anderson, © 2003 by Heinle & Heinle, a division of Thomson Learning, Inc. Reprinted by permission of the publisher.

"The Amazon Rainforest," from GLOBAL VILLAGE ENGLISH, by Matthew McGinniss.

本書構成與特色

　　本書針對克漏字、文意選填兩種大考必考題型設計，自國外書刊精心挑選 35 篇題材豐富的道地英語短文，內容包含：

克漏字（20 回）

◆ 10 題克漏字

一般學生在做克漏字練習時，常常只根據空格前後部分就判斷文章，忽略了上下文意應連貫的重要性，因此往往答題結束，仍不知文章所云為何。多樣化的文章設計，引起學生的學習興趣，讓學生除了可以練習克漏字外，亦可藉由閱讀文章並從中洞悉文章段落的組織架構，進一步培養最正確的克漏字解題方式。

◆ Extension 單元

深入分析克漏字的文法重點，並做系統性的延伸整理，克漏字必考句型、文法觀念一目了然。

文意選填（15 回）

　　完全參照大學學科能力測驗題型及出題方向，同時切合文章主題設計相關字彙整理小單元，不僅提高學習興趣，同時亦提昇學習的深度及廣度。

　　短文下方有字彙跑馬燈註解文章難字，夾冊附文章中譯與解析，適合用於課堂教學，亦可自修練習。

　　本書題目經精心設計，可根據文章前後文提供的線索，推測出生字及難字的意思。因此使用本書時，先別急著看字彙跑馬燈和文章中譯喔！建議讀者先完整閱讀文章一遍，若遇到生字或不懂之處，可依前後文先行猜測並做標記，等到作答完畢，再從解析及字彙跑馬燈中印證先前的推測，這樣才能增進閱讀能力、加深對單字的記憶力喔！

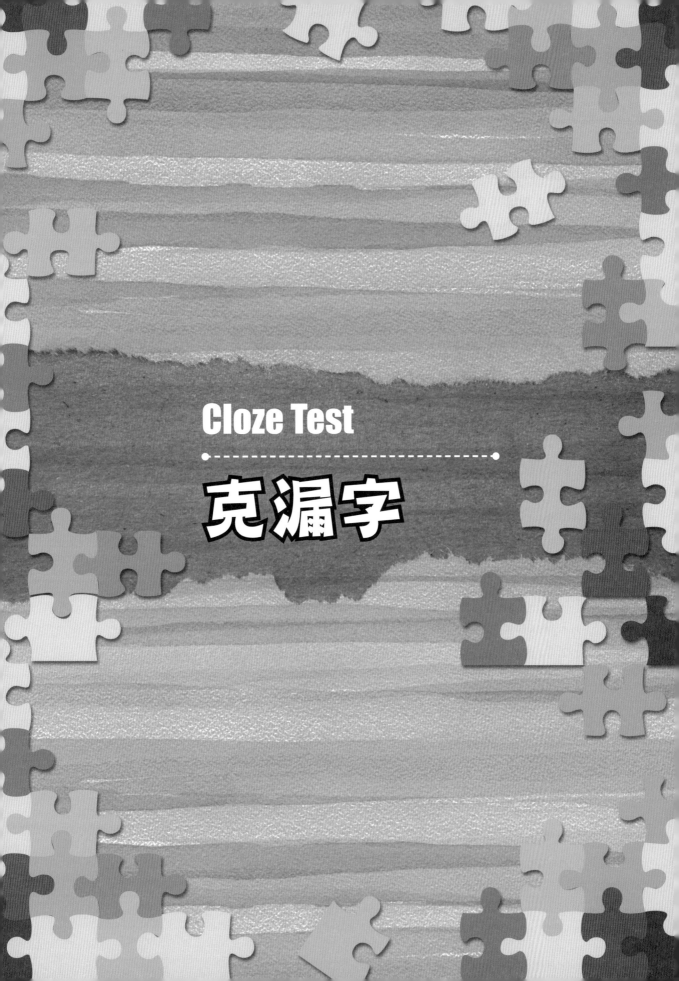

Cloze Test

克漏字

Food Personalities

People express their personalities in their clothes, their cars, and their homes. Because we might choose certain foods to "tell" people something about us, our ___1___ can also be an expression of our personalities. For example, some people eat mainly gourmet foods, ___2___ caviar and lobster. Moreover, they eat only in ___3___ restaurants (never in cafeterias or snack bars). They might want to "tell" the world that they know about the "better things in life."

Human beings can eat many different kinds of food, but vegetarians choose not to eat ___4___. They often have more in common than just their diet. Their personalities might be ___5___ too. For example, vegetarians in the United States may be creative people, and they might not enjoy competitive sports or jobs. They worry ___6___ the health of the world, and they probably don't believe in war.

Some people eat mostly "fast food." One study shows that many fast-food eaters have a lot in common with ___7___. However, they are very ___8___ from vegetarians. They are competitive and good ___9___ business. They are also usually in a hurry. Many fast-food eaters might not agree with this ___10___ of their personalities. Nonetheless, it is a common picture of them.

gourmet *adj.* (食品) 高級的　　caviar *n.* 魚子醬

(　) 1. (A) dialects　　(B) diets　　(C) designs　　(D) dyes

(　) 2. (A) namely　　(B) that is　　(C) such as　　(D) as

(　) 3. (A) cheap　　(B) small　　(C) common　　(D) expensive

(　) 4. (A) meat　　(B) fruit　　(C) vegetables　　(D) noodles

(　) 5. (A) similar　　(B) different　　(C) indifferent　　(D) strange

(　) 6. (A) with　　(B) about　　(C) for　　(D) within

(　) 7. (A) the others　　(B) the other　　(C) one another　　(D) each one

(　) 8. (A) separate　　(B) free　　(C) different　　(D) independent

(　) 9. (A) for　　(B) to　　(C) of　　(D) at

(　) 10. (A) prescription　　(B) subscription　　(C) inscription　　(D) description

Extension

such as 的用法

❶ **such as...** 如⋯，像是⋯

用來對前面所提的名詞 (人、事、物) 列舉物項，一般會舉出兩至三項。

◆ I've been to several countries in Europe, such as France, Germany and Switzerland.
我曾去過一些歐洲國家，像是法國、德國、瑞士等。

(※ France, Germany, Switzerland 都是前面 several countries in Europe 的舉例)

◎ 克漏字第 2 題的句子：

For example, some people eat mainly gourmet foods, such as caviar and lobster.
舉例來說，有些人吃的大多為美食，像是魚子醬和龍蝦。

注意 such as 可用 like 如⋯或 for example 例如代換，但前者多用於口語中，後者用於句中時，前後需有逗點隔開，亦可置於句尾。

❷ **such N as** 像⋯那樣的 N

◆ Here you can see such beautiful flowers as lilies, roses, and tulips.
在這裡你可以看見像百合花、玫瑰、鬱金香這樣美的花。

比較：Here you can see beautiful flowers such as lilies, roses, and tulips.
在這裡你可以看見美麗的花，例如百合花、玫瑰、鬱金香。

◆ Such a disaster as this had never happened to Sophia before.
Sophia 以前從未遭遇像這樣的災難。

③

Lie Detectors

A lie detector is a machine that is designed to show if a person is telling the truth. It does this by measuring a person's bodily reactions while he or she __1__. The machine records many body reactions while a person answers questions. It is __2__ the idea that stress produces changes in the body when a person does not tell the truth.

Taking a lie detector test __3__ placing several devices on different areas of a person's body. Rubber tubes on the chest and stomach record breathing. A device on the arm measures blood pressure. The body's reactions are recorded by another device.

__4__ a lie detector test, an expert first asks a series of questions. Then, the lie detector shows __5__ the person's body reacts when giving true and false answers. Then the expert asks the important questions. All this __6__ about two hours. Later, the expert reads the information and decides __7__ the person answered the questions truthfully.

There is much debate about the use of a lie detector. Many people do not believe it really can tell if a person is lying. The American Polygraph Association says a trained expert can tell most times if the person has __8__. But even that organization admits that mistakes __9__ sometimes.

The results of the test generally are not considered legal evidence in most United States courts. The Supreme Court has not __10__ ruled about the use of lie detector test results in the American legal system. However, some areas of the country have banned the use of lie detector tests as evidence.

polygraph = lie detector 測謊器　　ban v. 禁止

(　) 1. (A) has questioned　　　　　　　　(B) is being questioned
　　　　 (C) is questioning　　　　　　　　 (D) has been questioning

(　) 2. (A) based on　　　(B) on the base of　(C) according as　(D) based by

(　) 3. (A) interests　　　(B) introduces　　　(C) involves　　　(D) invites

(　) 4. (A) While　　　　(B) After　　　　　(C) Since　　　　　(D) During

(   ) 5. (A) how   (B) why   (C) what   (D) where

(   ) 6. (A) costs   (B) pays   (C) spends   (D) takes

(   ) 7. (A) that   (B) whether   (C) when   (D) what

(   ) 8. (A) laid   (B) lain   (C) lied   (D) lay

(   ) 9. (A) happen   (B) have   (C) are   (D) occur to

(   ) 10. (A) yet   (B) already   (C) just   (D) since

Extension

if 和 whether 的用法

I. 引導名詞子句，表「是否⋯」

◆ I don't know if/whether Bill will come on time tomorrow.

我不知 Bill 明天是否會準時前來。

◎ 克漏字第 7 題的句子：

...the expert...decides whether the person answered the questions truthfully.

⋯專家⋯判斷這個人是否誠實地回答問題。(※whether 可用 if 代替)

注意 whether 引導的名詞子句可做主詞、受詞、補語，但 if 引導的名詞子句只可做受詞

◆ Whether you join us is up to you.

你是否要加入我們由你決定。

(※ 此時 whether 引導的名詞子句做主詞，故不可用 if 代替)

II. 引導副詞子句

❶ **if**　假如⋯

純條件

◆ If it rains tomorrow, we will stay indoors.

如果明天下雨，我們將留在室內。

與現在／過去事實相反的假設

◆ If I were a millionaire, I could travel around the world.

假如我是百萬富翁，我就能環遊世界。(※與現在事實相反的 be 動詞一律用 **were**)

◆ If Linda had got up earlier this morning, she should have caught the train.

Linda 今早若早點起床，就應能趕上火車。(※實際上今早沒有早起)

❷ **whether...or...**　無論⋯或⋯

◆ Whether we go to your place or stay here, I really don't care.

無論我們去你家或是待在這裡，我真的沒意見。

注意 or 連接的兩個相對詞語若相同時，可省略後者，而 "or not" 亦可省略

◆ Whether you like it or not (like it), you have to do your homework.

= Whether you like it, you have to do your homework.

無論你喜不喜歡，你都必須做作業。

Androcles

Once upon a time a slave called Androcles escaped from his master and fled to the forest.

As he was wandering around there he found a lion __1__ moaning and groaning. __2__ he turned to run away, but seeing that the lion didn't chase him, he turned back and went up to him. As he approached, the lion put out his paw, which was all swollen and bleeding, and Androcles found that a huge thorn had got into it, and this was causing the lion's __3__. He pulled out the thorn and bound __4__ the paw of the lion, who was soon able to get up and lick Androcles' hand like a dog. Then the lion took Androcles to his cave, and __5__ him meat to eat every day.

But shortly afterwards both Androcles and the lion were captured, and the slave was sentenced to be thrown to a lion who __6__ any food for several days. The king and all his court came to see the spectacle, and Androcles was led out into the middle of the arena. Soon the lion was let loose from his den, and rushed to his victim, __7__.

But as soon as he came near to Androcles he __8__ his friend, and licked his hands like a friendly dog. The king was __9__ this and called Androcles to him, who told him the whole story. When he heard the story the king pardoned and __10__ the slave, and the lion was let loose into the forest.

Gratitude is the sign of noble souls.

| moan *v.*; *n.* 呻吟 | groan *v.*; *n.* 呻吟 | thorn *n.* 荊棘 | spectacle *n.* 精彩場面 |
| arena *n.* 競技場 | den *n.* 巢穴 | | |

(   ) 1. (A) laying down   (B) lied down   (C) lain down   (D) lying down

(   ) 2. (A) At first   (B) At last   (C) At least   (D) At large

(   ) 3. (A) happiness   (B) pain   (C) pride   (D) hunger

(   ) 4. (A) up   (B) to   (C) with   (D) by

(   ) 5. (A) provided   (B) took   (C) brought   (D) carried

(   ) 6. (A) wasn't given   (B) hadn't been given

       (C) hasn't eaten   (D) didn't eat

(　) 7. (A) bounding and roaring   (B) bounded and roared

       (C) to bound and roar   (D) bounding and roared

(　) 8. (A) refused   (B) recorded   (C) recognized   (D) reported

(　) 9. (A) amazed to   (B) amazed that   (C) surprised of   (D) surprised at

(　) 10. (A) released   (B) returned   (C) reminded   (D) relieved

Extension

表示「拿⋯，帶⋯」的動詞

❶ **bring** （從他處）帶來⋯
take （從說話者處）帶走⋯
fetch （去他處）取回⋯
carry 攜帶⋯，帶著⋯

◆ Have you brought an umbrella?
你有帶傘來嗎？

◆ Are you going to take your umbrella on today's hike?
今天的健行你打算帶傘去嗎？

◆ Go and fetch your umbrella.
去把你的傘拿來。

◆ I always carry my umbrella wherever I go.
無論到哪去，我總是隨身帶著傘。

❷ **bring, take, fetch** 皆可表示「帶某物給某人」，但語意依動詞本身的含意而不同。

$$\textbf{bring/take/fetch + sb. + sth.} \rightarrow \begin{cases} \textbf{bring/take + sth. + to + sb.} \\ \textbf{fetch + sth. + for + sb.} \end{cases}$$

◆ The waitress brought me a glass of water.
　　　　　　　　　　sb.　　sth.
服務生拿了杯水給我。(※從他處帶來)

◆ Please take these cookies to your sister on your way home.
　　　　　　sth.　　　　sb.
回家時請把這些點心拿給你姊姊。(※從說話者處帶走)

◆ I'll fetch the report for you.
　　　　　sth.　　　sb.
我會把報告拿來給你。(※去他處取回)

◎ 克漏字第 4 題句子：

The lion...brought him meat to eat everyday.
　　　　　　　sb.　sth.
獅子⋯每天拿肉給他吃。(※句型為 bring + sb. + sth.)

Netiquette—Internet Dos and Don'ts

Virginia Shea's book, *Netiquette*, lists a basic set of dos and don'ts for communicating appropriately with others in cyberspace. Following ___1___ some of her suggestions.

First, always remember that you are sending messages to a real person, not just to a computer. Don't type anything that you wouldn't say to someone's face. Also, remember that the person who receives your message cannot hear the tone of your voice, or see the ___2___ on your face. So, make sure your meaning is ___3___.

Don't do anything online that you wouldn't do in real life. Don't take anything without paying for it, ___4___ it's free. Don't read other people's e-mail—you wouldn't open your next-door neighbor's mailbox and open their mail, right? Do share your knowledge of the Internet with others. It's a big place ___5___ lots of information, and there are many new things to discover.

Remember that people judge you by your words and your actions, so do try to write well. Good writing skills, as well as correct grammar and spelling, ___6___. If you're uncertain about how to spell a word or which phrase to use, ___7___. There are lots of helpful books and websites.

It's okay to express your opinions online in forums ___8___ chat rooms or message boards, but don't start arguments with people. "Flame wars" in online discussions can be interesting to read, but ___9___ often unfair to other members of the group.

When you're online, just as in "real" life, try ___10___ other people's space, privacy, and feelings. Remember, you're not the only one traveling on this highway!

cyberspace *n.* 網路空間   forum *n.* 論壇

( ) 1. (A) is (B) has (C) are (D) have
( ) 2. (A) expression (B) impression (C) depression (D) oppression
( ) 3. (A) clean (B) clear (C) vague (D) ambiguous
( ) 4. (A) until (B) because (C) if (D) unless
( ) 5. (A) of (B) has (C) that is having (D) with

(   ) 6. (A) do matter   (B) does matter   (C) don't matter   (D) little matters

(   ) 7. (A) look it down   (B) look it up   (C) look at it   (D) see it off

(   ) 8. (A) as   (B) like   (C) such like   (D) include

(   ) 9. (A) maybe   (B) perhaps   (C) are   (D) is

(   ) 10. (A) remaining   (B) to remain   (C) respecting   (D) to respect

Extension

倒裝句

倒裝句是將句子的某一部分提至句首，並將主詞與助動詞或 be 動詞倒置，以達成「強調」目的的句子。

當句子為一般的 S + V 的結構時，很容易判別出與主詞對應的動詞。但是在遇到倒裝句時，需先在句中找到主詞，再判斷與之對應的動詞。

❶ 地方副詞——there, here, 或其他表方位、地點的介詞片語或副詞

◆ Here comes the bus.
      V   S

公車來了！(※主詞 the bus 與動詞 comes 倒置)

❷ 否定性副詞 (副詞片語、副詞子句)——hardly, scarcely, seldom, never... 等

◆ Never has Alisha gone abroad.
     aux. S

Alisha 不曾出國。(※主詞 Alisha 與助動詞 has 倒置)

❸ only 起首的副詞片語、副詞子句

◆ Only by working hard can we succeed.
             aux. S

只有靠努力不懈我們才能成功。(※主詞 we 與助動詞 can 倒置)

❹ so 起首的形容詞和副詞片語

◆ So nervous was Heather that she could not say a word.
         be   S

Heather 緊張得一句話都說不出來。(※主詞 Heather 與 be 動詞 was 倒置)

❺ 主詞補語——往往用於強調主詞補語或主詞太長時

◎ 克漏字第 1 題的句子：

結構為：Some of her suggestions are following
           S   be   SC

→ Following are some of her suggestions.
    SC   be   S

以下是她的一些建議。(※主詞 some of her suggestions 與 be 動詞 are 倒置)

American Attitudes Toward Work

Work is very important to most Americans. A job ___1___ provides them with a paycheck, but it also gives them a sense of identity. The first question that an American usually asks a person he has just met is, "What do you do?"

Work matters for most Americans. ___2___, it is something that they believe needs to come first, before almost anything else. They might not enjoy it, ___3___ they still believe that "work comes before play," or "business before pleasure." American students usually have this attitude toward school, too. For example, if American high school or college students on their way to class ___4___ a friend, they'll usually greet the friend, say a few words, and then say, "Well, I've got to go. I have a class." This is not impolite at all. If friends want to visit, they'll arrange ___5___ at another time, after class.

An American doesn't expect a friend to make a change in his or her work schedule to get together for a visit—either planned ___6___ accidental. Friends plan times to see each other when ___7___ one is working. It's impolite for people to expect a friend to be late ___8___ work or class—or to miss a day of work—in order to spend time together. This is, perhaps, especially true in the business world, ___9___ it is essential for people to show that they are responsible.

It's important to note that the ___10___ of work doesn't mean that work is more important to Americans than friendship is. It simply means that in terms of time and schedules, work usually comes before other things.

(   ) 1. (A) perhaps   (B) maybe   (C) not only   (D) by all means

(   ) 2. (A) That is   (B) As a result   (C) Such as   (D) For example

(   ) 3. (A) so   (B) for   (C) however   (D) but

(   ) 4. (A) run into   (B) come up with   (C) look into   (D) break into

(   ) 5. (A) meet   (B) meeting   (C) to meet   (D) to be met

(   ) 6. (A) and   (B) but   (C) or   (D) nor

(   ) 7. (A) each   (B) every   (C) either   (D) neither

(   ) 8. (A) in   (B) for   (C) to   (D) at

(   ) 9. (A) there   (B) in where   (C) in which   (D) and where

(   ) 10. (A) priority   (B) quality   (C) quantity   (D) personality

Extension

常用的連接詞片語

I. 兩者皆…

❶ **both A and B...** A 和 B 都… (※動詞對齊 AB 整體，故用複數形動詞)

◆ Both English and French are spoken in Quebec, Canada.

在加拿大的魁北克，英語和法語都有被使用。

❷ **not only A but also B...** 不僅 A 而且 B… (※重點在於 B，動詞與 B 看齊)

◆ Not only Tom but also his parents are proud of his achievement.

不僅是 Tom 自己，他的父母也都以他的成就為傲。

❸ **A as well as B...** 不僅 B 而且 A… (※重點在於 A，動詞與 A 看齊)

◆ The teacher as well as his students is looking forward to the summer vacation.

老師和學生都在期待暑假。

II. 兩者其中之一…

❶ **either A or B...** 不是 A 就是 B… (※動詞與 B 看齊)

◆ Either you or Bruce is to blame.

不是你就是 Bruce 該受責備。

❷ **A rather than B...** 是 A 而非 B… (※重點在於 A，動詞與看齊)

◆ The coach rather than the teammates is very ambitious.

是這位教練而不是隊友們懷抱雄心。

❸ **not A but B...** 不是 A 而是 B… (※重點在於 B，動詞與 B 看齊)

◆ Not Clark but you are responsible for this mistake.

要對這個錯誤負責的不是 Clark 而是你。

III. 兩者皆非…

neither A nor B... 既非 A 也非 B… (※動詞與 B 看齊)

◆ Neither you nor Rick is my best friend.

你和 Rick 都不是我最要好的朋友。

Elephants

Elephants are the largest land mammals in the world. They live on two continents, Africa and southern Asia. Asian elephants, also __1__ Indian elephants, are easier to tame than African elephants. The elephants you see in the circuses and zoos are nearly always Asian. African elephants are larger and have great ears like fans. Both the African and Indian elephants have strong, tough skin and long, lovely tusks. That is their problem. Elephants are __2__. People kill these animals in order to use their skin and their tusks. It is feared that by the end of the century, these huge mammals may be extinct. __3__, elephants are problems in some parts of Africa. In areas where the largest herds exist, they have become giant pests to the farmers. No fence is strong enough to keep these monsters away from the crops. Elephants go where they wish, __4__ food crops and farm buildings. African farmers wonder __5__ they can allow the elephants to continue to exist in their neighborhood.

Ten years ago, there were more than 1.3 million elephants in Africa. Over the past ten years, that number __6__ down to around 600,000. African elephants are hunted for their valuable ivory tusks. Most have been killed by poachers. Poachers are hunters who kill animals illegally. An adult elephant eats __7__ 300 pounds a day. In their search for food, elephants often move great distances. When they cannot find the grasses they prefer, they may strip the land __8__ trees.

Today, the area __9__ elephant herds live is much smaller than it used to be. Many areas in their path have been turned into farms. And some elephants have been killed by farmers for trampling their crops.

Our government has passed a law to protect the elephant. People cannot import or bring in items __10__ ivory or any part of the elephant's body. In addition, we need to promote the idea of protecting this creature by education.

mammal *n.* 哺乳類動物　　　tusk *n.* (象的) 長牙　　　extinct *adj.* 絕種的　　　poacher *n.* 偷獵者
trample *v.* 踐踏

(   ) 1. (A) known for   (B) known as   (C) knowing for   (D) knowing as

(   ) 2. (A) dangerous   (B) in danger   (C) endangering   (D) out of danger

(   ) 3. (A) However   (B) Therefore   (C) Besides   (D) Instead

(   ) 4. (A) destroyed   (B) destroy   (C) destroying   (D) to destroy

(   ) 5. (A) that   (B) when   (C) how   (D) if

(   ) 6. (A) has been cut   (B) is being cut   (C) have been cut   (D) are cutting

(   ) 7. (A) so much as   (B) so many as   (C) as much as   (D) as well as

(   ) 8. (A) from   (B) on   (C) off   (D) of

(   ) 9. (A) in which   (B) in that   (C) in where   (D) in there

(   ) 10. (A) are made from   (B) made from

         (C) making from   (D) which is made from

Extension

　　第三段最後一句中，用了一個特殊的及物動詞句型：strip + <u>sb.</u>/<u>sth.</u> + of...。類似用法的動詞如下：

❶ 從…奪取…

◆ Nothing can rob a man of his will.

士不可奪其志。(※**rob sb. of...**　從某人那裡奪取…)

◆ The farmer had to rid the garden of weeds.

農夫必須把花園的雜草除去。(※**rid <u>sb.</u>/<u>sth.</u> of...**　去除某人〔物〕的…)

◆ Worries deprived her of sleep.

煩惱使他失眠。(※**deprive sb. of...**　剝奪某人的…)

◎ 克漏字第 8 題的句子：

...they may strip the land of trees.

…牠們會將樹木從地上拔起。(※**strip <u>sb.</u>/<u>sth.</u> of...**　奪去某人〔物〕的…)

❷ 使某人得知…

◆ This picture reminded me of my family.

這張照片使我想起我的家人。(※**remind sb. of...**　使某人想起…)

◆ The weather bureau warned us of the coming typhoon.

氣象局警告我們有個颱風要來了。(※**warn sb. of...**　警告某人…)

◆ They informed me of your new address.

他們告知我你的新住址。(※**inform sb. of...**　通知、告知某人…)

◆ How can I convince you of my honesty?

我要怎樣才能使你相信我是誠實的？(※**convince sb. of...**　使某人充分相信…)

❸ 減輕某人的病痛

◆ The doctor has cured Lynn of her illness.

醫生治癒了 Lynn 的病。(※**cure sb. of...**　治癒某人的…〔病〕)

◆ This pill will relieve you of your headache.

這顆藥能紓解你的頭痛。(※**relieve sb. of...**　減輕某人的…〔痛苦〕)

At Home in a Cave

What's the most unusual kind of house that you have ever heard of? We all know that people lived in caves long ago. But did you know that nowadays thousands of people in southern Spain live in cave homes? In central Turkey, you can see whole villages of cave houses, some of ___1___ have lasted for nearly 2,000 years. And millions of people live in cave homes near the Yang-Tze River in China.

Living in these homes ___2___ more comfortable than you might think. They are naturally cool in summer and ___3___ in winter. The floors are often covered with tiles or rugs. The walls are painted. There are windows and doors. Many cave homes have telephones, and some ___4___ have fax and Internet connections. In Guadix, Spain, you can look out over a hillside that is covered with television antennas from the cave houses that lie beneath the surface.

Perhaps the most luxurious modern cave dwellings in the world can be found in the village of Troo, ___5___ in the Loire valley of France. For hundreds of years, the caves in this area have been used to store wine and grow mushrooms. In recent years, all the caves have been ___6___ modern conveniences like running water and electricity. There's even a restaurant that serves ___7___ meals. Today, many wealthy Parisians use the caves as second homes, since they provide a cool, relaxing change from the ___8___ of the city.

If you travel to some of these places, you can even find hotels that are in caves. In a village in Cappadocia, Turkey, ___9___, you can stay in an 11-room cave house carved out of the limestone rock. All the rooms come with private bathroom and telephone—a double room for a night ___10___ around US$50. You can get a unique experience of living in caves for a night or two.

tile *n.* 瓷磚   antenna *n.* 天線   dwelling *n.* 房屋   limestone *n.* 石灰岩

(   ) 1. (A) them   (B) those   (C) which   (D) that

(   ) 2. (A) are   (B) is   (C) have   (D) has

(   ) 3. (A) hot   (B) cold   (C) freezing   (D) warm

(   ) 4. (A) even   (B) ever   (C) never   (D) yet

(   ) 5. (A) situated   (B) locating   (C) stood   (D) situating

(   ) 6. (A) changed into   (B) fitted with   (C) covered with   (D) equipped by

(   ) 7. (A) 5-courses   (B) 5-courses'   (C) 5-course   (D) 5-course's

(   ) 8. (A) fast food   (B) slow movement

          (C) easy pace   (D) fast pace

(   ) 9. (A) for example   (B) in fact   (C) in addition   (D) that is

(   ) 10. (A) spends   (B) costs   (C) loses   (D) wastes

Extension

動名詞片語與不定詞片語

❶ 動名詞片語

動名詞與動名詞片語在句中可當**主詞**、**受詞**、或**補語**

當主詞	◆ **Eating too much** makes you fat. 吃太多使你發胖。 **注意** 動名詞片語當主詞時，動詞用**單數**
當受詞	◆ I enjoy **shopping**. 我喜歡購物。
當補語	◆ My hobby is **collecting stamps**. 我的嗜好是集郵。

❷ 不定詞片語

不定詞片語在句中可當**主詞**、**受詞**或**補語**

當主詞	◆ **To get up early** is a good habit. 早起是好習慣。 **注意** 不定詞片語當主詞時，動詞用**單數**
當受詞	◆ Christine likes **to play tennis**. Christine 喜歡打網球。
當補語	◆ Raven appears **to be rich**. Raven 好像很有錢。

◎ 克漏字第 2 題的句子：

Living in these homes is more comfortable than you might think.

住在這些房子裡頭比你想像的舒適。

(※因主詞為動名詞片語，故接單數動詞 is)

Lottery Winners—Rich, but Happy?

Every week, millions of dollars are spent, and won, on lottery tickets. The jackpot in many lotteries can be __1__ 100 million, and winners suddenly find themselves with more money than ever before. Many will have enough to purchase a new car, build a luxury house, take a holiday, and __2__ — all within a short amount of time. The lucky few who hit the jackpot, __3__, may end up with more problems.

Lottery organizers employ counselors to help jackpot winners. These counselors encourage winners __4__ from financial experts such as accountants, about how best to invest their money. The counselors also help winners to understand how their lives may change for the better — and possibly for the __5__. Luckily, many jackpot winners manage their fortunes sensibly. Some winners, however, do not use their money wisely and, __6__, end up in debt and struggling to make ends meet.

The biggest mistake many lottery winners make is overspending. A waiter who won $2 million in a California lottery spent all of his winnings shopping, having parties, and __7__ money to friends. A few months after he won, he was __8__ and working as a salesclerk.

__9__ large the jackpot is, there is always a risk that the money will run out if a winner overspends and does not invest wisely. Lottery winners should also remember they have to pay __10__ of their winnings to the government in taxes. So, even they became rich overnight, they should spend every penny with care.

lottery *n.* 彩券   hit the jackpot 中頭獎   counselor *n.* 顧問   make ends meet 達到收支平衡

( ) 1. (A) as much as   (B) as many as   (C) so much as   (D) so many as

( ) 2. (A) stop to work   (B) quit working   (C) not working   (D) start working

( ) 3. (A) therefore   (B) besides   (C) however   (D) at first

( ) 4. (A) getting advice   (B) to get advice
       (C) learn a lesson   (D) learning a lesson

( ) 5. (A) less   (B) more   (C) poorer   (D) worse

( ) 6. (A) as a result   (B) in fact   (C) on the contrary   (D) in addition

(   ) 7. (A) borrowing   (B) to borrow   (C) lending   (D) to lend

(   ) 8. (A) broke   (B) broken   (C) bankruptcy   (D) breaking

(   ) 9. (A) No matter   (B) No matter how   (C) Even if   (D) Whatever

(   ) 10. (A) a great number   (B) large quantity   (C) a big piece   (D) a large amount

Extension

表示「花費」的動詞

❶ **sb. spend + money/time +** $\begin{cases} \textbf{on N} \\ \textbf{(in) V-ing} \end{cases}$

spend 可同時用來指「金錢」、「時間」的花費

◆ Mary spent half of her salary on clothes.

= Mary spent half of her salary (in) buying clothes.

Mary 花了她薪水的一半買衣服。

◆ The boy spent his holiday on TV.

= The boy spent his holiday (in) watching TV.

那男孩把假期花在看電視上。

❷ **sb. pay + money + for N**

pay 常用於「金錢」的花費

◆ Sandy paid NT$3,000 for the ticket.

Sandy 花了三千元買票。

❸ **sb. take + time + to V = It take + (sb.) + time + to V**

take 常用於「時間」的花費

◆ We took five hours to get there. = It took us five hours to get there.

我們花了五個小時才到那裡。

❹ **sth. cost + (sb.) + money = It cost + (sb.) + money + to V**

cost 常用於「金錢」的花費

◆ The watch cost me NT$1,500.

= It cost me NT$1,500 to buy the watch.

買這隻錶花了我一千五百元。

On the Road: Travel Lifestyles

Just as people have different lifestyles at home, their ways of living "on the road" vary, too. Some travelers prefer to __1__ in big hotels, eat at expensive restaurants, and concentrate on the most famous tourist sights. __2__ believe that sightseeing is just one reason to travel — not the only reason. They want to be able to get to know a variety of people and to understand different opinions, values, and problems; to do so, they meet other travelers at inexpensive hotels, camping places, and so on. __3__, they try to learn about new places by paying attention to people in restaurants, public parks, shopping centers, entertainment areas, and the like.

__4__ other travelers prefer to get to know the cultures of the places they are visiting by spending time with natives of the areas. A few even stay in the private homes of families there. How is it possible to do this? Various international organizations provide educational experiences for people who want to discover lifestyles __5__ their own. Through programs __6__ the American Field Service, the Experiment in International Living, travel exchanges, language courses, and the like, visitors can learn about life in other places. Participants in such programs are usually students who get to know the natives during homestays of several weeks, months, or __7__ a year.

Of course not all travelers have a lot of time for long homestays; __8__, there are also opportunities for tourists with only short vacations to exchange information and opinions with the natives of an area. One of the organizations which provides such opportunities __9__ Servas International. It has been bringing together people of different national, religious, cultural, and financial backgrounds __10__ many years. This group gives travelers the chance to meet people all over the world.

participant *n.* 參與者

(   ) 1. (A) living   (B) live   (C) staying   (D) stay

(   ) 2. (A) Others   (B) Another   (C) The other   (D) Each other

(   ) 3. (A) However   (B) Instead   (C) Therefore   (D) Moreover

(   ) 4. (A) Still   (B) Some   (C) More   (D) Most

(　　) 5. (A) differ from　　(B) different from　(C) the same with　(D) similar to

(　　) 6. (A) as well as　　(B) such as　　　(C) include　　　　(D) other than

(　　) 7. (A) ever　　　　　(B) only　　　　　(C) even　　　　　(D) for

(　　) 8. (A) for example　(B) as a result　　(C) nevertheless　　(D) on the contrary

(　　) 9. (A) called　　　　(B) calling　　　　(C) to call　　　　(D) is called

(　　) 10. (A) in　　　　　(B) for　　　　　(C) since　　　　　(D) till

Extension

prefer 的用法

❶ prefer $\begin{cases} \textbf{to + V} \\ \textbf{V-ing} \end{cases}$ 偏好做…

◆ I prefer studying at night.

我喜歡在晚上讀書。

◎ 克漏字第 1 題的句子：

Some travelers prefer to stay in big hotels....

有些旅行者偏好住大型的旅館…。

❷ prefer + that 子句　偏好…

◆ We prefer that you keep silent.

我們比較喜歡你保持沈默。

❸ prefer A to B　喜好 A 甚於 B

◆ I prefer tea to coffee.

我喜歡茶甚於咖啡。

◆ Gordon prefers watching TV to going to the movies.

Gordon 喜歡看電視甚於看電影。

注意 當 A、B 是不定詞片語 to + V 時，可用 rather than 代替原句型中的 to

　　◆ She prefers to stay rather than (to) go.

　　　她比較想留下來，不想去。

❹ prefer N + $\begin{cases} \textbf{to + V} \\ \textbf{adj.} \end{cases}$ 希望 N…

◆ I prefer you to come later.

我希望你待會來。

◆ I prefer my steak well-done.

我的牛排要全熟。

New Zealand

New Zealand consists of two main islands. One is North Island, and ___1___ is South Island. The former features ___2___ volcanoes, while the latter experiences colder weather and has a landscape of mountains with snow and glaciers. All over these two islands, there ___3___ many fresh water lakes and rivers that run down to the Pacific Ocean.

___4___ else in the world can so many of its plants and animals be found because the country is isolated in the ocean. The most famous and a popular symbol of the country is the Kiwi bird which is nocturnal and can't fly. New Zealand is also home to the Kauri Tree which stands thirty meters tall and lives for ___5___ two thousand years. Much of the country is covered in national parks that give protection to forests and wildlife.

The first people to live in New Zealand were the Maori people who came from nearby islands one thousand years ago. Two centuries ago, Europeans ___6___ by the British arrived to establish colonies. Today the Maori culture remains ___7___ and blends well with the cultures of people who have come from all parts of the world to live in New Zealand. The population of New Zealand is nearly four million, ___8___ most people living on North Island.

New Zealand is known ___9___ a paradise for nature lovers. It is also a great place for people ___10___ outdoor activities such as hiking and skiing. This combination of the modern and friendly culture of the people makes New Zealand a popular country to visit.

glacier *n.* 冰河　　nocturnal *adj.* 夜行性的　　wildlife *n.* 野生生物

(　　) 1. (A) another 　　　(B) other 　　　　(C) the other 　　　(D) the second
(　　) 2. (A) a series of 　(B) a flock of 　　(C) a school of 　　(D) a big sum of
(　　) 3. (A) have 　　　　(B) has 　　　　　(C) are 　　　　　(D) is
(　　) 4. (A) Somewhere 　(B) Nowhere 　　(C) Anywhere 　　(D) Everywhere
(　　) 5. (A) as far as 　　　(B) as long as 　　(C) as soon as 　　(D) as old as
(　　) 6. (A) that are led 　(B) leading 　　　(C) who was led 　(D) led

(　　) 7. (A) strong   (B) strongly   (C) strength   (D) strengthen

(　　) 8. (A) when   (B) because   (C) with   (D) having

(　　) 9. (A) like   (B) as   (C) about   (D) by

(　　) 10. (A) enjoy   (B) enjoyed   (C) enjoying   (D) who enjoys

Extension

with 的用法

❶ with 最常解釋為「和…一起」

◎ 本文第三段第三句：

Today the Maori culture...blends well with the cultures of people who have come from all parts of the world....

而今，毛利文化…和來自世界各地的人帶來的各種文化充分融合…。

❷ 有著…，帶著…

◆ The girl with long hair lives in the house with a red roof.

這長髮女孩住在紅色屋頂的房子。

◆ I always carry an umbrella with me.

我總是隨身攜帶傘。

❸ 以…，用…——表工具、手段等

◆ He struck me with a stick.

他用棍子打我。

❹ 由於…，因為…——表原因、理由

◆ Gracie is in bed with a fever.

Gracie 因發燒而臥床。

❺ 在…的狀態下——引導表附帶情況的片語

◆ Don't speak with your mouth full.

嘴巴裝滿食物的時候不可以說話。(※在滿嘴食物的狀態下)

◆ How lonely I will feel with you away!

你不在，我會有多麼寂寞啊！(※在你不在的狀態下)

◎ 克漏字第 8 題的句子：

The population of New Zealand is nearly four million, with most people living on North Island.　紐西蘭人口大約四百萬人，大多數人都住在北島。

(※with 不用刻意翻譯出來，表示附帶情況)

The Call of the East

Doris Brougham was born in Seattle to a Christian family and was one of nine children. When she was 11 years old, she attended a summer camp __1__ a minister from China spoke about his ancient land. __2__ hearing his lecture, Brougham decided that when she grew up, she was going to China as a missionary.

In 1948, the 21-year-old Brougham __3__ her dream of becoming a trumpeter and her scholarship to New York's Eastman School of Music. Choosing instead to become a missionary, she boarded a ship for the __4__ journey to China, passing through Tokyo, Busan, Manila and Hong Kong before arriving in war-torn Shanghai. China's civil war forced her __5__ to Chongqing, Lanzhou and Hong Kong, before finally coming to Taiwan with her church.

When Brougham arrived here, she noted that there were few people on the east coast and many towns without churches. She therefore decided to __6__ her mission in Hualien.

She began teaching music at Yu-Shan Theological College and Seminary in Hualien in 1951 and was also responsible for training the school's Sunday school teachers. She soon __7__ a small church and put together her own small Sunday school class. She taught her Sunday school students about the Christian faith, and at the same time, __8__ some of the language of the aborigines of the area. Whenever the children invited her to their homes, she always used her just-acquired language, __9__ her odd accent. The families at first thought it strange to hear her __10__ them in their own language. However, in the end her efforts brought smiles to their faces.

missionary *n.* 傳教士	theological *adj.* 神學的	aborigine *n.* 原住民

(   ) 1. (A) at where   (B) at which   (C) there   (D) and where

(   ) 2. (A) When she   (B) Since   (C) On   (D) Because

(   ) 3. (A) gave up   (B) turned down   (C) built up   (D) realized

(   ) 4. (A) six-weeks   (B) six-weeked   (C) six weeks'   (D) six-week

(   ) 5. (A) flee   (B) fled   (C) fleeing   (D) to flee

( ) 6. (A) set up   (B) get up   (C) end up   (D) make up

( ) 7. (A) published   (B) established   (C) accomplished   (D) abolished

( ) 8. (A) picking up   (B) picked up   (C) using up   (D) used up

( ) 9. (A) instead of   (B) for fear of   (C) in spite of   (D) in addition to

( ) 10. (A) greeted   (B) greets   (C) greet   (D) to greet

Extension

複合形容詞

本文出現多個複合形容詞，如 21-year-old (二十一歲的)、 six-week (六週的)、 war-torn (戰亂的)、 just-acquired (剛學會的) 等。複合形容詞的種類如下：

❶ **number – 單數單位名詞**

例：a ten-day vacation 十天的假期　　a five-dollar coin 五元硬幣

❷ **adj. – N + ed**

例：a one-eyed man 獨眼人　　a kind-hearted person 心地善良的人

❸ **adj. – 連綴動詞 + ing**

連綴動詞指 look、taste、sound、smell... 等字。

例：a sour-tasting apple → an apple that tastes sour 味道酸的蘋果
　　　　　　　　　　　　　　　　　　　　連綴 V　adj.

　　a nice-looking girl → a girl who looks nice 好看的女孩
　　　　　　　　　　　　　　　　　連綴 V　adj.

❹ **N – 及物動詞 + ing (主動關係)**

例：a man-eating tiger → a tiger that eats man 吃人的老虎
　　　　　　　　　　　　　　　　　　vt.

　　a labor-saving machine → a machine that saves labor. 省勞力的機器
　　　　　　　　　　　　　　　　　　　　vt.

❺ **adv. – 不及物動詞 + ing (主動關係)**

例：a south-going train → a train that goes south 南下的火車
　　　　　　　　　　　　　　　　　　vi.

　　a slowly-walking man → a man who walks slowly 慢慢走的男子
　　　　　　　　　　　　　　　　　　　vi.

❻ **N – p.p. (被動關係)**

例：a heart-broken girl → a girl whose heart is broken 傷心的女孩
　　　　　　　　　　　　　　　　　　　　　被動

　　a man-made fiber → a fiber which is made by man. 人造纖維
　　　　　　　　　　　　　　　　　　　被動

❼ **adv. – p.p. (被動關係)**

例：a well-trained sportsman → a sportsman who is well trained 訓練有素的運動員
　　　　　　　　　　　　　　　　　　　　　　　被動

　　a deeply-moved reader → a reader who is deeply moved 深受感動的讀者
　　　　　　　　　　　　　　　　　　　　　　被動

Formal Letter Writing: A Dying Art?

Needless to say, the speed and ease of using the Internet has changed our lives. Nowadays, sending e-mail— __1__ mailing letters using the postal system (now often called "snail mail")—is the preferred means of communication for most people.

In a survey of 2,000 young people __2__ the e-mail provider MSN Hotmail, around half said they send thank-you notes by e-mail, not post. __3__ sending more personal e-mail, young people entering the working world today find themselves sending and replying to hundreds of business related e-mails every week.

However, many of these same young people seem to be unaware of some basic rules when it comes to __4__ e-mail at work. Most of the people __5__ to the survey said they didn't check their spelling or punctuation before hitting "send." Even more surprising was __6__ one in twenty of the survey's respondents said they sometimes send e-mails to their boss with the words "love and kisses!" This is normally considered inappropriate workplace etiquette.

The main reason for this use of __7__ language in workplace e-mail is that a lot of young people have always communicated with others on the Internet—especially using social networking services—in a relaxed and friendly manner. For many, online communication outside of work __8__ talking with others in chat rooms, posting on message boards, and sending e-mail to friends. They are all __9__ .

With more business correspondence now being conducted using the Internet than ever before, it is important for people to be __10__ of the differences in language use between personal and business communication—especially when using e-mail. People should always remember to show politeness while dealing with business e-mails.

punctuation *n.* 標點符號　　　　respondent *n.* 回答者　　　　etiquette *n.* 禮儀
correspondence *n.* 信函　　　　conduct *v.* 進行

(　　) 1. (A) ✕ (B) and (C) or (D) rather than

(　　) 2. (A) conducting (B) conducted by

(C) who are conducted by (D) that is conducting

(　　) 3. (A) In spite of (B) Because of (C) In addition to (D) With a view to

(　　) 4. (A) sending (B) send (C) receiving (D) receive

(　　) 5. (A) responding (B) responded (C) to respond (D) respond

(　　) 6. (A) that (B) what (C) which (D) ✕

(　　) 7. (A) important (B) informal (C) immortal (D) inconvenient

(　　) 8. (A) include (B) exclude (C) involves (D) including

(　　) 9. (A) in vain (B) on purpose (C) on business (D) for fun

(　　) 10. (A) proud (B) afraid (C) in favor (D) aware

Extension

to 當介系詞的用法

　　to 後面常接原形動詞，構成不定詞，然而在克漏字第 3、4 題中，to 為介系詞，後需接名詞或動名詞。以下為幾個常見的這類用法：

I. 構成介系詞片語

❶ **in addition to + N/V-ing**　除了⋯

◆ In addition to <u>playing</u> golf, Stanley likes to go fishing.

除了高爾夫球，Stanley 還喜歡釣魚。

❷ **with a view to + N/V-ing**　為了⋯

◆ We had a meeting with a view to <u>discussing</u> the problem.

我們為了討論該問題而召開會議。

II. 構成動詞片語

❶ **be used to + N/V-ing**　習慣於⋯

◆ I am used to <u>paying</u> with a credit card.

我習慣用信用卡付帳。

❷ **devote oneself to + N/V-ing**　致力於⋯

◆ Tina devoted herself to <u>teaching</u> English.

Tina 致力於英語教學。

❸ **look forward to + N/V-ing**　期待⋯

◆ I'm looking forward to <u>seeing</u> you.

我期待見到你。

III. 和動詞連用

❶ **object to + N/V-ing**　反對⋯

◆ The new CEO proposed a whole new operating plan, but the board objected to changing the origin one.

新執行長提案了全新的經營計畫，但董事會反對改變原來的計畫。

Are eSports Really Sports?

People love to compete, and throughout history we see instances of that taking place. Games were created to test the skills and strength of those __1__ them. Quite often, people would compete __2__ one another in sports games in the hope of becoming champions. These games were __3__ popular __3__ events like the Olympics were eventually formed. The desire to play in sports games, and for spectators to watch them, has long been part of human history.

Today, technology is redefining what sports games mean. In the world of video games, there are now professional "athletes" __4__ compete against each other and draw large audiences that want to watch them play. These players can compete in solo event or play as part of a team, just like in the Olympic Games. However, __5__ going through serious physical training to prepare for the competition, these video game athletes hone their skills by watching a video screen.

Those who reach the top level and are able to compete in video game competitions are professional. Basically, this means that there is enough prize money to be won for the players to __6__ by doing it. In Taiwan, these players often join the Taiwan eSports League (TeSL).

__7__ in 2008, TeSL brought professional video game competitions to the television screen. The players are paid a base salary, and they live together in a team house. Like athletes, they have an inner drive to win.

__8__ the popularity of eSports, the Taiwanese government has not recognized eSports as an official sport. One of the objections raised is that eSports are not Olympic sports, and therefore shouldn't be __9__ part of the sports industry. However, other countries have recognized eSports as __10__ sports, and some members of Taiwan's government have shown support for such official recognition. What the future holds for eSports is yet to be determined.

spectator *n.* 觀眾　　hone *v.* 磨練

(   ) 1. (A) plays   (B) playing   (C) played   (D) play

(   ) 2. (A) to   (B) in   (C) against   (D) from

(   ) 3. (A) so; that   (B) too; to   (C) as; as   (D) such; that

(   ) 4. (A) who   (B) whom   (C) which   (D) whose

(   ) 5. (A) because of   (B) owing to   (C) according to   (D) rather than

(   ) 6. (A) stay up   (B) put off   (C) make a living   (D) bump into

(   ) 7. (A) Founding   (B) Founded   (C) Founder   (D) Founds

(   ) 8. (A) Except   (B) Besides   (C) From   (D) Despite

(   ) 9. (A) regarded   (B) seen   (C) viewed   (D) considered

(   ) 10. (A) legal   (B) classical   (C) initial   (D) frequent

Extension

「A 被認為是 B」的句型

A be considered/thought (to be) B

= A be thought of/seen/viewed/regarded as B　A 被認為是 B

　　本句型用來表示「A 被認為是 B」，共有兩種句型可以使用，其中 B 是主詞補語，可以是「名詞」或「形容詞」。這兩種句型之間存在著一些差異，在第一種句型當中，在 considered 或 thought 後面要接 to be，而且可以省略。在第二種句型當中，在 thought of 和 regarded 等後面要接介系詞 as，但是不能省略。另外必須注意的是，在兩種句型中所使用的動詞並不相同，不能混用，請務必牢記每一個動詞所屬的句型是哪一個。

◆ Tracy is considered (to be) the smartest student in her class.

　　= Tracy is regarded as the smartest student in her class.

　　Tracy 被認為是班上最聰明的學生。

　　(※以 the smartest student 這個名詞片語當作主詞補語)

◆ The problem of air pollution in this city is thought (to be) quite serious.

　　= The problem of air pollution in this city is viewed as quite serious.

　　這個城市裡的空氣污染問題被認為相當地嚴重。

　　(※以 quite serious 這個形容詞片語當作主詞補語)

　　注意 這個句型也可以轉變為主動語態：

S consider/think A (to be) B = S think of/see/view/regard A as B

　　同樣地，在第一種句型當中的 to be 可以省略，而在第二種句型當中的介系詞 as 則是不能省略的。

◆ We consider Janet (to be) a genius.

　　= We view Janet as a genius.　我們認為 Janet 是一個天才。

◎ 克漏字第 9 題的句子

One of the objections raised is that eSports are not Olympic sports, and therefore shouldn't be considered part of the sports industry.

人們所提出的反對意見之一是，電子競技不是奧運的競技項目，因此不應該<u>被認為是</u>運動產業的一部分。

Salmon

Atlantic salmon are hatched in freshwater rivers that flow into the Atlantic Ocean. The salmon remain in freshwater rivers precisely two years, feeding constantly until they are about nine inches __1__, and then they begin swimming downriver. The trip downriver is a tough journey. Many immature salmon are caught by predators including humans and bears, before __2__ the ocean. Those that survive the journey and make it to the Atlantic swim far out to the shallow banks around the island of Greenland, __3__ they feed for two or three years, growing sometimes to weights of twenty pounds or more.

At the age of four or five, the salmon return to their original hatching grounds to spawn. Scientists cannot explain why they return, __4__ explain why all salmon return at once. __5__, no one knows how they make it. Unless the salmon __6__ by fishermen or other predators, they swim to the headwaters, spawn, and return to the ocean again.

Despite the ceaseless urge that drives the salmon and despite the salmon's "courage," this cycle is a fragile one. In the early nineteenth century, __7__, the Connecticut River was full of these fish, but the last one was caught in 1874. The modern world humans created had destroyed the salmon's __8__. Power dams were built, which disturbed the fish and kept them __9__ swimming upstream to their spawning grounds. Industries dumped __10__ into the Connecticut, along with hot waste water that made the river impossible for the fish. The Atlantic salmon disappeared from the Connecticut River, and they disappeared from almost all the New England waterways.

salmon *n.* 鮭魚	freshwater *adj.* 淡水的	predator *n.* 掠食者	spawn *v.* (魚等) 產卵
fragile *adj.* 脆弱的			

(   ) 1. (A) old   (B) long   (C) tall   (D) deep

(   ) 2. (A) they arrive   (B) they reach at

        (C) reaching   (D) getting along with

(   ) 3. (A) that   (B) which   (C) where   (D) there

(   ) 4. (A) nor can they   (B) nor they can   (C) hardly can they (D) they can never

(   ) 5. (A) In conclusion   (B) In advance   (C) In consequence (D) In fact

(   ) 6. (A) are caught   (B) is caught   (C) are brought up   (D) is brought up

(   ) 7. (A) for one thing   (B) for instance   (C) for good   (D) for sure

(   ) 8. (A) experiment   (B) government   (C) assignment   (D) environment

(   ) 9. (A) from   (B) in   (C) with   (D) by

(   ) 10. (A) population   (B) pollution   (C) proportion   (D) property

Extension

單複數同形的名詞

　　有些同學以為字尾加 "s" 的是複數名詞，沒加 "s" 的就是單數名詞，其實並不盡然，本文就有單複數同形的字 "fish" 和 "salmon"，在本文它們皆當複數名詞，代名詞皆用 "they"。類似的名詞還有很多，例如：deer (鹿)、sheep (羊)、series (系列)、species (品種)、corps (軍團)、gross (籮)、aircraft (航空器)、Chinese (中國人)、Japanese (日本人)⋯等。這類名詞的用法如下：

◆ The hunter saw a deer running among the bush.
　獵人看到一隻鹿在灌木叢間奔跑。

◆ The skillful hunter shot three deer last week.
　那位高明的獵人上週打了三隻鹿。

(※一隻鹿用 a deer，三隻鹿不需在字尾加 s)

nor 的用法

❶ 與 neither 或 not 連用，表「既不⋯也不⋯」

◆ It is neither hot nor cold.
　天氣既不熱也不冷。

◆ Not a man nor a child is to be seen here.
　這裡看不到大人，也看不到小孩。

❷ 用於否定句後，表示連續否定

注意 nor 後的句子必須倒裝

◆ I haven't been to Japan, nor have I wanted to go there.
　我從未到過日本，也從不想去那裡。

◎ 本文第二段第二句：

Scientists cannot explain why they return, nor can they explain why all salmon return back at once.
科學家無法解釋鮭魚為何會回去，也無法解釋為何所有的鮭魚都同時回去。

Human Endurance—What the Body Can Survive

Athletes push themselves to the limits of physical and mental endurance by regularly trying to go faster, higher, and further in their chosen sport than any other athlete did in the past. In doing this, many athletes risk ___1___ themselves. Many spend weeks or months recovering from damage they have ___2___ to their bodies while in training.

The world's finest athletes gather at the Olympic Games ___3___ four years. At this event, they demonstrate both their athletic skill and their strength. At the Sydney Olympics in 2000, a British athlete—Steve Redgrave—showed the world ___4___ the human mind and body could do. Redgrave won Olympic gold medals for rowing in 1984, 1988, 1992, and 1996, ___5___ nine World Championship golds. He was one of the best athletes in his sport.

During the long training periods ___6___ the Sydney Olympics, Steve had numerous health problems. He had surgery for appendicitis in 1997, and in 1998 he was diagnosed with diabetes. This meant that he had to give himself daily injections of insulin to help him ___7___ his blood sugar. ___8___ giving up rowing—a very physically demanding sport—Redgrave chose to continue the exhausting training necessary for the Olympics. ___9___ his body was sick, he didn't want to surrender.

At the Sydney Games Steve and his team rowed to victory, and his fifth Olympic gold medal. It was an amazing achievement for Redgrave, who proved to the world how determination can help one to cope with and ___10___ an illness. Until now, he is still the only person who have won gold medals at five Olympics in an endurance sport.

endurance *n.* 耐力	appendicitis *n.* 盲腸炎	diagnose *v.* 診斷	diabetes *n.* 糖尿病
injection *n.* 注射	insulin *n.* 胰島素		

(   ) 1. (A) injuring   (B) to injure   (C) injuries   (D) injured

(   ) 2. (A) made   (B) done   (C) given   (D) taken

(   ) 3. (A) every   (B) within   (C) in   (D) for

(   ) 4. (A) how   (B) that   (C) what   (D) why

(   ) 5. (A) as well as   (B) except for   (C) as long as   (D) in the hope of

(   ) 6. (A) that leads up to (B) lead to   (C) led up to   (D) leading up to

(   ) 7. (A) controlled   (B) control   (C) controlling   (D) with control

(   ) 8. (A) In spite of   (B) In addition to   (C) Instead of   (D) In case of

(   ) 9. (A) Until   (B) As if   (C) Only when   (D) Even though

(   ) 10. (A) suffer from   (B) overcome   (C) win   (D) overlook

 **Unit 15**

Extension

every 表示「每隔⋯」

every + other + 單數時間名詞

every + two, three... + 複數時間名詞

◆ Oliver has to go to the hospital every other day (= every two days).

Oliver 每隔一天就必須去醫院。(※即「每兩天一次」)

◎ 克漏字第 3 題的句子：

The world's finest athletes gather at the Olympic Games every four years.

全世界最傑出的運動員每四年齊聚於奧林匹克運動會。

複合關係代名詞 what

what = { the thing(s) which / that which / all that }　　what = 先行詞 + 關係代名詞

◆ A person is usually judged by what (= the things that) he or she does.

人常以自身所做的事被加以論定。

◆ Alfie is not an honest man. I don't believe what (= that which) he said.

Alfie 並不是個誠實的人，我不相信他說的。

◆ Oscar is very honest. You can believe what (= all that) he tells you.

Oscar 非常誠實，你可以相信他告訴你的每句話。

◎ 克漏字第 4 題的句子：

...Steven Redgrave...showed the world what (= the things which) the human mind and body could do.

⋯史蒂夫・雷德格瑞夫⋯向全世界展示人體身心的能耐 (所能做的事)。

The Amazon Rainforest

Located in South America, the Amazon Rainforest, the greatest expanse of rainforest on earth, spreads across nine countries and covers an area half the size of Europe. It __1__ not only the mighty Amazon River but also millions of species of insects, birds, animals, plants and trees.

So huge is the Amazon Rainforest that it has direct effects __2__ global weather patterns. It serves as the lungs of the earth, producing a large percentage of the oxygen that people and animals need __3__. The forest also prevents global warming __4__ a balanced atmosphere. For these reasons, the value of the rainforest cannot be measured in money terms, but __5__ it is actually measured in this way.

Many of the tree species that produce hard wood have been chopped down and sold in international markets. Parts of the forest have been burnt down and __6__ non-native trees. These newly-planted trees are used to __7__ rubber and paper. Other parts of the forest have been burnt down simply to provide more fields for farmers to graze their cattle. __8__ the forest has been destroyed like this, the soil becomes badly damaged and the land starts to erode.

People everywhere are concerned that the Amazon Rainforest __9__ destroyed. Awareness of the problem is high, but people continue to ruin the forest for their own commercial gain. However, in reality the forest contains so many resources that it is impossible to expect people and companies __10__. The best we can hope for is that when the forest's resources are used, they are done so in a way that doesn't do permanent damage to one of the world's most valuable assets.

expanse *n.* 廣闊區域　　graze *v.* 放牧　　erode *v.* 侵蝕　　asset *n.* 資產

(　　) 1. (A) composes　　(B) consists　　(C) makes up of　　(D) contains

(　　) 2. (A) to　　(B) with　　(C) for　　(D) on

(　　) 3. (A) to breathe　　(B) breathe　　(C) breathing　　(D) to be breathed

(　　) 4. (A) from helping maintain　　　　(B) by helping maintain

　　　　　(C) to help maintaining　　　　　(D) helping the maintenance of

( ) 5. (A) fortunately   (B) unfortunately   (C) accordingly   (D) consequently

( ) 6. (A) replaced with   (B) substituted for   (C) provided with   (D) changed by

( ) 7. (A) producing   (B) production   (C) produce   (D) making

( ) 8. (A) Before   (B) Until   (C) Once   (D) Although

( ) 9. (A) is being   (B) has   (C) had been   (D) was being

( ) 10. (A) taking advantage of it   (B) to take advantage of it

       (C) leaving it alone   (D) to leave it alone

Extension

so...that... 的用法

so...that... 如此…以致於…

so 與其後的形容詞、副詞可提至句首，形成倒裝句型

$$S + \begin{Bmatrix} be\ 動詞 \\ V \end{Bmatrix} + so + \begin{Bmatrix} Adj. \\ Adv. \end{Bmatrix} + that\text{-}clause$$

$$= So + \begin{Bmatrix} Adj. \\ Adv. \end{Bmatrix} + \begin{Bmatrix} be\ 動詞 + S \\ 助動詞 + S + 原形\ V \end{Bmatrix} + that\text{-}clause$$

倒裝句型

◆ Mandy is so nervous that she could not say a word.

= <u>So nervous is Mandy</u> that she could not say a word.
　　　　倒裝

Mandy 緊張得一句話都說不出來。

◆ Timmy works so diligently that he often forgets to eat dinner.

= <u>So diligently does Timmy work</u> that he often forgets to eat dinner.
　　　　倒裝

Timmy 勤奮工作以致於常忘記吃晚餐。

◎ 本文第二段第一句：

<u>So huge is the Amazon Rainforest</u> that it has direct effects on global weather patterns.
　　　　倒裝

亞馬遜雨林極其廣闊，以致於對全球的氣候型態有直接影響。

(※以 so huge 起首，be 動詞提至主詞 the Amazon Rainforest 前，形成倒裝句型)

Online Shopping—Convenient and Fun

In today's busy world, shoppers like convenience. That's one reason ___1___ online shopping has experienced a recent boom worldwide, and online businesses are making huge profits. You can now buy a stylish dress from France, book a flight to Tokyo, or order a pizza from a local restaurant online ___2___ a simple click of a button on your mobile device.

Three recent surveys indicated that more and more consumers around the world are shopping online, ___3___ shopping in person in stores remains the most popular way to purchase items. More consumers are also shopping globally, ___4___ products from international businesses and ___4___ them faster.

One survey indicates that more than 60 percent of Taiwanese Internet users shop online, spending an ___5___ of NT$16,586 per person yearly. Sixteen percent of Taiwanese Internet users also sell products online. The most popular online purchases among Taiwanese shoppers ___6___ clothing, tours and hotel reservations, airline tickets, event tickets, and grocery supplies. Taiwanese consumers say they shop online because they like the convenience ___7___ with the ability to read reviews of products before purchasing them.

Although customers value convenience, most of them aren't going to spend money without ___8___ a good deal. Consumers want to purchase the right product from the right place at the right time and at the right price. The Internet ___9___ a vast range of products and services for consumers to compare. And best of all, the doors to this virtual store are open ___10___! Customers can enjoy the convenience of online shopping anytime and anywhere.

| boom *n.* 迅速發展 | worldwide *adv.* 全球地 | stylish *adj.* 流行的 | purchase *v.*; *n.* 購買 |
| virtual *adj.* 虛擬的 | | | |

( ) 1. (A) for   (B) which   (C) where   (D) that

( ) 2. (A) to   (B) from   (C) with   (D) between

( ) 3. (A) since   (B) although   (C) after   (D) whether

( ) 4. (A) ordered; received   (B) ordering; received

    (C) ordered; receiving   (D) ordering; receiving

( ) 5. (A) average (B) extent (C) impression (D) output

( ) 6. (A) was (B) has (C) are (D) is

( ) 7. (A) combines (B) combining (C) combined (D) combination

( ) 8. (A) getting (B) gotten (C) gets (D) got

( ) 9. (A) adapts (B) offers (C) omits (D) desires

( ) 10. (A) on and off   (B) from a distance

    (C) sooner or later   (D) around the clock

Extension

although/though 引導的讓步子句

❶ **Although/Though S + V, S + V** 雖然…，但是…

由 although/though 所引導之讓步子句，在中文裡譯為「雖然…但是…」。不過要注意的是，受到中文的影響，許多人在使用這個句型時常會把 although/though 和 but 連用。然而，在英文當中這兩者其實是不能連用的。也就是說，如果句子裡用了 although/though 的話，就不能用 but；同樣地，如果用了 but，就不能用 although/though。

◆ Although/Though Richard is wealthy, he never looks down upon the poor.

= Richard is wealthy, but he never looks down upon the poor.

雖然 Richard 很富裕，但是他從不會瞧不起貧窮的人。

◎ 克漏字第 3 題的句子

Three recent surveys indicated that more and more consumers around the world are shopping online, although shopping in person in stores remains the most popular way to purchase items.

雖然親自到店裡選購仍然是最受歡迎的購物方式，但是三項最近的調查指出，全世界有越來越多的人正在進行網路購物。

❷ **In spite of/Despite + N/V-ing, S + V** 雖然…但是…

我們也可以把 although/though S + V 的句型替換為此句型，但此處必須要注意的是，although 和 though 是連接詞，故後面要接完整的子句，而 in spite of 和 despite 是介系詞，故後面要接名詞或動名詞片語當作受詞。若要在這兩種句型之間轉換的話，要特別注意這一點。

◆ Although it rained heavily, the baseball game was not cancelled.

= Despite the heavy rain, the baseball game was not cancelled.

雖然下起了大雨，但是這場棒球賽並未被取消。

Vitamins

Vitamin research may be the fastest growing area of research in medicine. __1__ the fact that the public trusts vitamins to do exactly what their manufacturers say they will do and rushes to buy vitamins, there are a great many misunderstandings and myths about what vitamins are and how consumers should use them. And research has proven these myths wrong.

First of all, many vitamins simply will not do __2__ is often claimed. Vitamin C has never been proven to aid in the prevention of colds. B vitamins do not __3__ tiredness. Any effect a person feels when taking a B-12 capsule, __4__, is purely a psychological effect. B-12 deficiencies are rare, and even in cases where B-12 treatment is necessary, the vitamin must be injected because it is ineffective when __5__ orally.

Vitamin E is often said to prevent heart disease, improve virility, and slow the aging __6__. However, the fact that male rats become sterile when lacking in vitamin E doesn't mean the same thing __7__ humans who have the same problem.

The most common vitamins are A, B-1, B-2, C, and D; and if you eat a balanced diet that __8__ these vitamins, it's unnecessary for you to take any other vitamin pills. Though many people claim that you should eat special foods or take vitamin pills daily to make sure you are getting the correct quantity of vitamins, this is simply not true. __9__, you may take in too much of vitamins by doing this. Some vitamins are toxic if you take in too much of them. The truth is that vitamin __10__ is often more severe than vitamin deficiency. Moreover, it's becoming more common.

myth *n.* 迷思   capsule *n.* 膠囊   deficiency *n.* 缺乏   inject *v.* 注射
virility *n.* 男性生殖力   sterile *adj.* 不孕的

(   ) 1. (A) Thanks to   (B) Because of   (C) In spite   (D) Despite

(   ) 2. (A) the thing   (B) that   (C) which   (D) what

(   ) 3. (A) get rid of   (B) give up   (C) get along with   (D) put up with

(   ) 4. (A) as a result   (B) for example   (C) in conclusion   (D) for one thing

(   ) 5. (A) to take   (B) taking   (C) taken   (D) it takes

(   ) 6. (A) process   (B) access   (C) program   (D) project

(   ) 7. (A) belongs to   (B) happens to   (C) refers to   (D) compares with

(   ) 8. (A) protects   (B) prevents   (C) provides   (D) consists

(   ) 9. (A) Actual   (B) That is   (C) In fact   (D) To sum up

(   ) 10. (A) overwork   (B) overweight   (C) overcoat   (D) overdose

Extension

分詞構句

若主要子句與副詞子句的主詞相同時，可改為分詞構句：

Ⅰ. 將從屬子句的動詞改為分詞

❶ 動詞與主詞為主動關係時，改為現在分詞

◆ When she asked me for a loan last week, she promised to return it to me in three days.

(※she 和 ask 的關係為主動)

→ When asking me for a loan last week, ...

她上週向我借錢時，答應三天內還我。

❷ 動詞與主詞為被動關係時，改為過去分詞

◆ The actress smiled and shook her head when she was asked if she had a good boyfriend.

(※ she 和 ask 的關係為被動)

→ ...when asked if she had a good boyfriend.

被問到有沒有要好男友時，這位女演員微笑搖頭。

◎ 克漏字第 5 題的句子：

...it is ineffective when taken (= it is taken) orally.

…口服時它的效果不彰。(※ it 指 vitamin，和 take 的關係為被動)

Ⅱ. 若副詞子句的動詞是 be 動詞，其主詞可以和 be 動詞一併省略

◆ Though (we were) poor, we lived a happy life.

我們雖然窮，但生活得很快樂。

◆ While (he was) young, he lived with his grandparents in the countryside.

他年輕時，和祖父母一起住在鄉間。

Understanding More About AIDS

AIDS, a biologically complex disease that destroys the human immune system, is spreading across the world. Every day nearly sixteen thousand people contract the virus called HIV, ___1___ finally turns into AIDS. As there is still no cure ___2___ AIDS, people who have the disease will certainly die from it. It is therefore very important for people to understand more about the disease. ___3___, the spread of AIDS will hopefully be curbed when people know how to take the correct precautions.

The AIDS virus is carried in human blood. When someone is exposed to another person's blood, he or she may also be exposed to the AIDS virus. There are three main ways ___4___ AIDS is spread. The most common way is through ___5___ contact with someone who already has the disease. Unprotected sex is dangerous because when a person has sex with someone else, he or she will be exposed to not just one person but to all the other people his or her partner has had sex with. ___6___ the AIDS disease enters a community, it will spread quickly to many other people.

When people use needles for drugs or other purposes, they also risk ___7___ the disease. By sharing a needle with another person, a drug user comes directly ___8___ other blood. If one of these people has AIDS, it is likely that the other person will also get AIDS. The third way to catch AIDS is through blood transfusion. If a person is in an accident and needs blood, there is a chance that the blood he or she ___9___ will carry AIDS. This way of contracting AIDS is rare now. In poorer countries, ___10___, this is still a danger. Because blood donors are hardly tested for AIDS, those blood receivers are at risk.

biologically *adv.* 生物 (學) 地	immune system *n.* 免疫系統	curb *v.* 控制
precaution *n.* 預防措施	be exposed to... 接觸到…	transfusion *n.* 輸血

(　　) 1. (A) who　　(B) which　　(C) it　　(D) that

(　　) 2. (A) from　　(B) of　　(C) for　　(D) on

(　　) 3. (A) In this way　　(B) In no way　　(C) By the way　　(D) On the way

(　　) 4. (A) in which　　(B) where　　(C) when　　(D) why

(   ) 5. (A) social   (B) usual   (C) natural   (D) sexual

(   ) 6. (A) Though   (B) Once   (C) Until   (D) Unless

(   ) 7. (A) to contract   (B) to contact   (C) contracting   (D) contacting

(   ) 8. (A) in contact with   (B) in comparison with

             (C) in return for   (D) with regard to

(   ) 9. (A) donates   (B) returns   (C) removes   (D) receives

(   ) 10. (A) for example   (B) in other words   (C) therefore   (D) however

Extension

關係副詞 when、where、why、how

❶ 關係代名詞的用法與其前的先行詞有關，先行詞是「人」時用 who，先行詞是「事、物」時用 which。關係副詞連接**形容詞子句**時，其用法亦與前面的先行詞 (時間、地方、理由、方法) 有關：

時間	**when**	I don't know <u>the time</u> **when** (= at which) he will arrive. 我不知道他到達的時間。
地方	**where**	This is <u>the place</u> **where** (= in which) I was born. 這就是我出生的地方。
理由	**why**	She didn't tell me <u>the reason</u> **why** (= for which) she burst into tears the day before. 她沒告訴我她前天突然大哭的原因。
方法	**how**	The cook refused to tell us <u>the way</u> **how** (=in which) he made the delicious dish. 這位廚師不肯告訴我們這道美味的菜是怎麼做的。 **注意** how 多以 **in which** 或 **that** 代替

◎ 克漏字第 4 題的句子：

There are three main ways in which AIDS is spread.

愛滋病傳播途徑主要有三種。

(※因先行詞 ways 指方法，故用經常取代 how 的 in which)

❷ 關係副詞前的先行詞可省略，形成**名詞子句**，句意不變。

框內例句可改為：

◆ I don't know when he will arrives. (※省略 the time)

◆ This is where I was born. (※省略 the place)

◆ She didn't tell me why she burst into tears the day before. (※省略 the reason)

◆ The cook refused to tell us how he made the delicious dish. (※省略 the way)

Illustrated Literature

The relationship between art and literature dates back thousands of years. Before printed literature had become widely available, stories were ___1___ orally. However, paintings were also an enormously valuable form of storytelling. They helped to keep myths and legends ___2___ through the ages. Today, illustrations ___3___ an important role in many forms of literature from poetry in magazines to children's fiction and graphic novels for adults.

Picture books for young children provide a good example of ___4___ text and illustration are closely interconnected. Child psychologists have shown that pictures are important for kids who are learning to read. In fact, even picture books without words may help very young children to read by ___5___ the notion of a "self that reads." For adults, an increasingly popular form of illustrated literature is the graphic novel. These comic books ___6___ mainly intended for teenagers but nowadays many adults are reading them too. The themes explored in graphic novels range ___7___ light humor to profound philosophy. Illustrations in children's books and graphic novels are gaining recognition as a serious form of visual art that deserves ___8___ much respect ___8___ traditional forms like painting and sculpture. ___9___ prestigious international awards have been established to honor the best illustrators in the publishing industry.

The marriage between illustration and literature continues to ___10___ as artists and writers explore the possibilities of their relationship. The digital revolution has given illustrators and writers new freedom to work together and express their creativity. In the future, more and more illustrated literature will be available to readers online as well as in traditional book form.

myth *n.* 神話	graphic *adj.* 圖像的	interconnect *v.* 互相連結	notion *n.* 概念
profound *adj.* 深奧的	prestigious *adj.* 有聲望的		

(   ) 1. (A) passed away   (B) passed by   (C) passed on   (D) passed out

(   ) 2. (A) asleep   (B) alive   (C) alone   (D) awake

(   ) 3. (A) take   (B) play   (C) have   (D) do

(　　) 4. (A) how　　　　　(B) what　　　　　(C) which　　　　　(D) that

(　　) 5. (A) developed　　(B) develops　　　(C) development　　(D) developing

(　　) 6. (A) used to be　　　　　　　　　　(B) are used to being

　　　　　(C) were used to be　　　　　　　　(D) are used as being

(　　) 7. (A) upon　　　　　(B) with　　　　　(C) from　　　　　(D) into

(　　) 8. (A) more; than　　(B) so; that　　　(C) enough; for　　(D) as; as

(　　) 9. (A) The number of (B) An amount of (C) The amount of (D) A number of

(　　) 10. (A) hover　　　　(B) evolve　　　　(C) shoplift　　　　(D) plunge

Extension

used to 的用法

❶ used to + V　過去曾經或經常…

用來表示「過去曾經做過的事或狀態」或是「過去經常做的事」，但是本片語強烈暗示該動作或狀態現在已經消失或是出現完全不一樣的情況。

◆ My father used to eat a large amount of meat when he was young, but now he has become a vegetarian.

我爸爸過去年輕時經常吃大量的肉，但是他現在已經成為素食主義者了。

(※用 used to + V 表主詞過去常做的事，而後半句則表示現在已經變為不同情況)

◎ 克漏字第 6 題的句子：

These comic books used to be mainly intended for teenagers but nowadays many adults are reading them too.

這些漫畫書過去主要是給青少年看的，但是現在許多成年人也看這些漫畫書。

❷ be used to + V　被用來…

本句型意思是「某物被用來做…」，表示某物的「用途」，在 to 後面要接原形動詞，而本句型另外還有一個意義相同的類似句型：be used for N/V-ing，但是在 for 後面要接名詞或動名詞，而不是接原形動詞。

◆ This device is used to transform sunlight into electricity.

= This device is used for transforming sunlight into electricity.

這個裝置被用來把陽光轉換為電力。

❸ be used to N/V-ing　習慣於…

本句型用來表示某人的某個習慣，請注意在此句型中的 to 是介系詞，故後面要接名詞或動名詞片語，記得不要和 be used to + V 的用法搞混了。另外，本句型中的 used 可以用 accustomed 來替換，意思與用法完全一樣。

◆ Beatrice is used/accustomed to finishing her homework before going to bed.

Beatrice 習慣在上床睡覺前完成回家作業。

Cloze Test

文意選填

The Salt Merchant and His Ass

One day a merchant who dealt in salt drove his ass to the seashore to buy salt. His road home __1__ across a stream. When passing it, his ass made a false step and fell __2__ into the water. The ass rose up again with his load lighter, as the water __3__ the salt. The merchant returned to the seashore and loaded his ass with a larger __4__ of salt than before. When coming again to the stream, the ass fell down __5__ in the same spot. Then, he regained his feet with the weight of his load much __6__. The merchant saw through his prank, and drove him for the __7__ time to the coast. He __8__ a cargo of sponges instead of salt. When he reached the stream, the ass again tried to play the __9__. He fell down by intention, and the sponges became swollen with the water. His load was very greatly __10__, giving his back a doubled burden. He got the punishment he deserved.

從下列選項中選擇最適當者填入空格中：

(A) on purpose	(B) increased	(C) bought	(D) by accident	(E) lay
(F) melted	(G) quantity	(H) decreased	(I) third	(J) trick

1. _____   2. _____   3. _____   4. _____   5. _____

6. _____   7. _____   8. _____   9. _____   10. _____

regain v. 恢復	see through 看穿	prank n. 惡作劇	sponge n. 海綿
by intention 故意地	swollen adj. 腫脹的		

Language Note

本篇選自伊索寓言 (Aesop's Fables)，用驢子 (ass) 來比喻愚笨的人。其他常用來比喻人的動物還有：

▶ wolf n. 狼；殘忍的人

▶ weasel n. 黃鼠狼；狡猾的人

▶ snake n. 蛇；陰險的人

▶ lion-hearted adj. 勇敢的

▶ as sly as a fox (狐狸般) 狡猾的

▶ as gentle as a dove (鴿子般) 溫馴的

The Ways to Prevent "Burnout"

Many of us face "burnout" at some point in our lives. It can be prevented, ___1___, if you take action before placing yourself at risk.

First, you must decide what is really important in your life, and make time for the people and activities most ___2___ to you.

Second, you need to ___3___ your feelings with others. Express your frustrations, disappointments, and painful experiences, ___4___ joys and accomplishments. If you do not do this regularly, you could "explode." Nurturing healthy relationships with others will strengthen you and bring greater ___5___ to your life.

Third, make sure you have time off. Take short breaks and regular ___6___, whether you feel you need them or not. Learn how to say "no" ___7___ you can say "yes" to the things that are really important to you. Find activities to fill and elevate your spirit, ___8___ music, dance, sports, massage, or meditation. And schedule time to be alone sometimes.

Finally, seek the right ___9___ if you need help and all else has failed. There is no ___10___ in this. What's more, it may be what you need to restore your spiritual well-being.

從下列選項中選擇最適當者填入空格中：

(A) such as	(B) balance	(C) share	(D) doctor	(E) meaningful
(F) so that	(G) however	(H) shame	(I) vacations	(J) as well as

1. _____   2. _____   3. _____   4. _____   5. _____

6. _____   7. _____   8. _____   9. _____   10. _____

nurture *v.* 養育   elevate *v.* 提升   meditation *n.* 冥想   well-being *n.* 健康

Language Note

本文末段中合適的醫生指精神科醫生 (psychiatrist)。其他類別的醫生有：

▶ physician *n.* 內科醫生   ▶ surgeon *n.* 外科醫生

▶ dentist *n.* 牙醫   ▶ pediatrician *n.* 小兒科醫生

Encouragement

Dante Gabriel Rossetti was a famous 19th-century poet and artist. He was once approached by an elderly man who had some drawings that he wanted Rossetti to have a __1__ at and tell him if they were any good.

Rossetti looked them over carefully. After the first few, he knew that they were worthless, showing not the least sign of artistic talent. But Rossetti was a kind man, and he told the elderly man the truth as gently as __2__ . He said that the pictures were without much value and showed __3__ talent. He was sorry, but he could not __4__ to the man.

The visitor was disappointed, but seemed to expect Rossetti's judgment. He then apologized for __5__ Rossetti's time, but would he just look at a few more drawings—these done by a young art student?

Rossetti looked over these drawings and immediately became excited about the talent they revealed. "These," he said, "oh, these are good. This young student has __6__ talent. He should be given every help and encouragement in his __7__ as an artist. He has a great future if he will work hard and stick to it."

Rossetti could see that the old man was __8__ moved. "Who is this fine young artist?" he asked. "Your son?"

"No," said the old man sadly. "It is me—40 years __9__ . If only I had heard your __10__ then! For you see, I got discouraged and gave up—too soon."

從下列選項中選擇最適當者填入空格中：

(A) taking up	(B) praise	(C) deeply	(D) career	(E) look
(F) ago	(G) great	(H) little	(I) possible	(J) lie

1. _____   2. _____   3. _____   4. _____   5. _____

6. _____   7. _____   8. _____   9. _____   10. _____

Bats

The evil reputation of bats is easy to understand. These creatures have been accused of attacking humans and carrying infectious ___1___. The fact that they sleep during the day and fly at night also adds to their ___2___. However, bats do not attack humans. Actually, there are more deaths each year from pet dog attacks and bees than from bats.

Bats perform an important ecological ___3___ throughout the world. They eat millions of harmful insects yearly. The food a bat eats every night, ___4___, amounts to one quarter of its own body weight. A single colony of Arizona bats observed by scientists eat ___5___ 35,000 pounds of insects every night. That's the equivalent ___6___ of 34 elephants!

Bats may soon disappear from the world because, ___7___, they are fast losing their natural homes—caves, abandoned mines, certain kinds of trees. Bats are also in danger from certain chemicals used by farmers to fight ___8___ insects. Scientists have found that in the State of Arizona alone, the number of bats has ___9___ from 30 million to 30,000 over the past six years. Many people kill bats out of ___10___ fear. Said one bat expert, "The most critical need for bat conservation today is increased public awareness and education."

從下列選項中選擇最適當者填入空格中：

| (A) mystery | (B) destructive | (C) weight | (D) diseases | (E) unreasonable |
| (F) declined | (G) in fact | (H) up to | (I) for one thing | (J) function |

1. _____   2. _____   3. _____   4. _____   5. _____

6. _____   7. _____   8. _____   9. _____   10. _____

infectious *adj.* 傳染性的 ecological *adj.* 生態的 equivalent *adj.* 相等的 in danger 處於危機中

Obesity

Far too many people are overweight. Obesity may be the most serious health problem facing Americans today because it is a contributing ___1___ to so many other health problems. Heart and artery system disease, diabetes, high blood ___2___ and arthritis are more common in people who are overweight. Extra weight causes problems with muscles and joints. Many studies are beginning to ___3___ cancer with obesity, for cancer cells are more likely to be found in fat tissue than in muscle.

Overweight people may suffer mentally ___4___ their health problems. People who are overweight find it ___5___ to buy clothes. People who are significantly overweight find public facilities such as airline seats or waiting room chairs too ___6___. Some obese people say they feel humiliated by their condition, so they avoid going out ___7___. Some overweight people avoid exercise because their extra ___8___ makes exercise difficult. As their activity decreases, it becomes easier to ___9___ weight. It's because exercise would have "burned off" ___10___ some calories. Thus, many obese people get caught in this vicious circle of exercising less and gaining weight.

從下列選項中選擇最適當者填入空格中：

(A) at least	(B) in public	(C) in addition to	(D) pressure	(E) cause
(F) link	(G) small	(H) gain	(I) weight	(J) difficult

1. _____   2. _____   3. _____   4. _____   5. _____

6. _____   7. _____   8. _____   9. _____   10. _____

obesity *n.* 肥胖	artery *adj.* 血管的	arthritis *n.* 關節炎
humiliated *adj.* 難堪的	calorie *n.* 卡路里 (熱量單位)	vicious circle *n.* 惡性循環

Language Note

本篇討論「肥胖」的人所遭遇到的問題，常用來形容人肥胖的字有：

▶ obese *adj.* 肥胖的 (常用於醫學上)　　▶ flabby *adj.* (肌肉) 鬆弛的；肥胖的

▶ chubby *adj.* (孩童、嬰孩) 胖嘟嘟的　　▶ stout *adj.* (中年人) 發福的

The Story of Pele

Edson Arantes do Nascimento, better known as Pele, was born on October 23, 1940. His family ___1___ in a small village in Brazil, and they were very poor. Edson learned to play soccer when he was very young. He used whatever he could find as a ball, even a grapefruit or a ball of rags.

When Edson was 8, one of the children playing soccer gave him the nickname "Pele" for no ___2___. The word didn't mean anything, so Edson thought it was a(n) ___3___. Soon the name caught on, and other kids started ___4___ him "Pele." Edson would fight the other kids to stop ___5___ until he was suspended for two days from school. The name stuck, however, and it wasn't long before even his parents called him Pele.

When Pele was 11, a trainer named Waldeman de Brito observed him playing ___6___ soccer. Brito kept his eye on Pele, and four years later, brought him to Santos to train as a professional. At first, Pele's teammates were ___7___ at Brito's faith in Pele. But Pele proved himself time and again. Over his career, Pele ___8___ 1281 goals in 1363 matches. He played in four FIFA World Cups, winning three. Once, people in Nigeria stopped their ___9___ war for 48 hours so Pele could play in an exhibition match in the capital. Since then, Pele became known as the man who stopped war.

Pele retired in 1974. Since then, Pele has used his resources to help people in need and ___10___ friendship between countries through soccer competition. In 1994, Brazil appointed him "Minister of Sport," which enables him to serve the world by sport continually.

從下列選項中選擇最適當者填入空格中：

(A) scored	(B) teasing	(C) insult	(D) civil	(E) reason
(F) amateur	(G) lived	(H) surprised	(I) promote	(J) calling

1. _____   2. _____   3. _____   4. _____   5. _____

6. _____   7. _____   8. _____   9. _____   10. _____

catch on 變得流行   suspend v. 使休學

Language Note

和足球比賽相關的字有：

▶ goal *n.* 球門；得分

▶ score a goal （足球）得到一分

▶ goalkeeper *n.* 守門員

▶ referee *n.* 裁判

▶ red card *n.* 紅牌 (表示判罰出場)

▶ yellow card *n.* 黃牌 (表示警告)

Robots

What comes into your mind when you think about robots? Do you imagine armies of evil metal monsters planning to take over the world? Or, perhaps of mechanical men who have been created as guards or soldiers by a mad genius. Or maybe you think of ___1___ robots who act, think, and look like human beings. In fact, robots like these have more to do with science fiction films than with real life. In the real world robots are machines that do jobs which ___2___ have to be done by people. Robots operate either ___3___ or under the control of a person.

In a car factory, ___4___, robot machinery can put together and paint car bodies. On the seabed, remote controlled ___5___ machines with mechanical arms can perform tasks. Those tasks are too difficult for ___6___. Robot spacecraft can explore the solar system and ___7___ back information about planets and stars.

Many robots have computer brains. Some robots are fitted with cameras, sensors, and ___8___ which enable them to see, to feel, and to hear. And some robots can even produce electronic speech.

All this does not mean that a robot can think and ___9___ like a human being. Present-day robots have to be programmed with a good deal of information before they can ___10___ even simple tasks. In other words, it's impossible for robots in real world to think independently like those in the movies or science fiction up to now.

從下列選項中選擇最適當者填入空格中：

| (A) underwater | (B) send | (C) otherwise | (D) by themselves | (E) behave |
| (F) microphones | (G) man-like | (H) carry out | (I) divers | (J) for example |

1. _____   2. _____   3. _____   4. _____   5. _____

6. _____   7. _____   8. _____   9. _____   10. _____

take over... 接管…   seabed *n.* 海底   spacecraft *n.* 太空船   solar system 太陽系
sensor *n.* 感應器

Hope Emerges as Key to Success in Life

Psychologists are finding that hope plays a surprisingly important role. It gives people a great advantage in ___1___ like academic achievement, bearing with difficult jobs and coping with tragic illness. And, ___2___, the loss of hope is turning out to be a strong sign that a person may commit suicide.

"Hope has proven a powerful predictor of outcome in every study we've done ___3___." said Dr. Charles R. Snyder, a psychologist at the University of Kansas. He has ___4___ a scale to assess how much hope a person has.

People who get a high score on the hope scale "have had ___5___ hard times as those with low scores, but have learned to think about it in a hopeful way, seeing a setback as a challenge, not a failure," Dr. Snyder said.

He found that people with high levels of hope share several ___6___ :

· They turn to friends for advice on how to ___7___ their goals.

· They tell themselves they can succeed at what they need to do.

· Even in a difficult situation, they tell themselves things will get ___8___ as time goes on.

· If hope for one goal fades, they aim for ___9___ .

· They show an ability to break a tough task into ___10___ , achievable parts.

With these traits, people tend to make a success in life.

從下列選項中選擇最適當者填入空格中：

(A) characteristics	(B) as many	(C) another	(D) aspects	(E) devised
(F) specific	(G) so far	(H) by contrast	(I) achieve	(J) better

1. _____   2. _____   3. _____   4. _____   5. _____

6. _____   7. _____   8. _____   9. _____   10. _____

bear with... 忍耐   predictor *n.* 預測指標   assess *v.* 評估   setback *n.* 挫折

World Water Council—To the Rescue of Water

The World Water Council is an organization made up of members from all over the world. Its ___1___ is to discuss better ways to conserve, protect, and manage fresh water around the world. It has tried to teach these ___2___ to all of the governments, large companies, and other important people that make major decisions concerning water problems around the world.

So many successful international meetings were held to ___3___ water problems between governments. In 1995, a(n) ___4___ committee was created to decide what the aims of the World Water Council would be. It was then ___5___ formed in June, 1996. Its main ___6___ is set up in the city of Marseilles, France.

Most of the World Water Council's main activities are to hold special meetings that bring important people and experts ___7___ together. The World Water Council also tries to make sure that fresh water is available to everyone around the world and works hard to ___8___ water to poor countries. It has formed many groups, such as the Water Cooperation Facility, and used the money from its ___9___ to help reduce water problems around the world.

The conservation and protection of fresh water is ___10___ to people of the world. Most governments have recognized this need and are actively helping make the projects of the World Water Council successful.

從下列選項中選擇適當者填入空格中：

(A) techniques	(B) headquarters	(C) officially	(D) membership	(E) bring
(F) purpose	(G) solve	(H) crucial	(I) worldwide	(J) particular

1. _____   2. _____   3. _____   4. _____   5. _____

6. _____   7. _____   8. _____   9. _____   10. _____

conserve v. 節省

The Highway Winding Through Taroko Gorge

The Central Cross-Island Highway was completed in 1960. It cost __1__ billions of dollars to build. Also, it cost the lives of the 212 __2__. They __3__ during its construction. Their sacrifice will never be __4__.

The section of the Central Cross-Island Highway that runs __5__ Taroko Gorge is carved from sheer cliffs. It offers __6__ views of mountains, curving tunnels, and heart-stopping glimpses into the gorge.

There's one thing to __7__ when riding along this section of the highway. That is, __8__ as it is, it's just another highway to the countless truckers who use it regularly to haul things across the island. Time is __9__ to truckers. As a result, don't be surprised when they blow past you at full __10__. Be careful of yourself while enjoying the magnificent views.

從下列選項中選擇最適當者填入空格中：

| (A) workers | (B) forgotten | (C) more than | (D) speed | (E) beautiful |
| (F) money | (G) breathtaking | (H) remember | (I) died | (J) through |

1. _____   2. _____   3. _____   4. _____   5. _____

6. _____   7. _____   8. _____   9. _____   10. _____

wind v. 蜿蜒   gorge n. 峽谷   sheer adj. 陡峭的   haul v. 運送

Language Note

本文提到 gorge (峽谷)、cliff (山壁) 等地形，其他相關的地形名詞有：

▶ peak n. 山峰
▶ summit n. 山頂
▶ ridge n. 山脊
▶ valley n. 山谷
▶ range n. 山脈

First Aid

The major causes of death in America today are heart attack and sudden injury. Most people have been, or will be, present when a victim of one of these sudden attacks ___1___ for an ambulance. If the victim loses pulse and breathing, the chances for ___2___ fall tremendously. Only 18 percent survive if no one can help the victim to maintain pulse and ___3___ until an ambulance arrives.

If, ___4___, the victim receives vital aid within the first minute, there is a 98 percent chance to stay alive. As aid arrives later and later, these chances ___5___. After four minutes without a pulse, ___6___, the brain begins to deteriorate. If help is delayed for six minutes, the victim's chances ___7___ to 11 percent. It is vitally important that all of us understand the ___8___ to take when someone's pulse or breathing stops suddenly.

Of all ___9___, 50 percent are caused by choking. If a victim struggles to take air into his or her lungs, immediately check for blockage in the mouth or throat. Sometimes, a wheezing noise indicates that the airway is partially blocked, and the victim can't breathe normally. An absence of noise is ___10___ more serious. It indicates a completely blocked airway, which may cause the victim's death soon.

從下列選項中選擇最適當者填入空格中：

(A) deaths	(B) fall	(C) however	(D) waits	(E) survival
(F) decrease	(G) even	(H) breathing	(I) in fact	(J) measures

1. _____ 2. _____ 3. _____ 4. _____ 5. _____

6. _____ 7. _____ 8. _____ 9. _____ 10. _____

ambulance *n.* 救護車　　　pulse *n.* 脈搏　　　deteriorate *v.* 惡化　　　blockage *n.* 阻塞物
wheeze *v.* 喘息　　　airway *n.* 氣管

Language Note

以下是一些需要 first aid (急救) 的狀況：

- ▶ choke *n.*; *v.* 窒息
- ▶ drown *v.* 溺水
- ▶ stroke *n.* 中風
- ▶ poisoning *n.* 中毒
- ▶ shock *n.* 休克，電擊
- ▶ burn *n.*; *v.* 灼傷

- ▶ asthma *n.* 氣喘
- ▶ fracture *n.*; *v.* 骨折
- ▶ heart attack　心臟病發作
- ▶ heat stroke　中暑
- ▶ heat exhaustion　熱衰竭
- ▶ get/receive an electric shock　觸電

For Your Dark Hours

"There is not enough darkness in all the world to put out the light of one small candle."

During the last war I heard Cecil Roberts, the British novelist, tell me how he found those __1__ on a small new gravestone outside a blitzed British town. And how he searched in vain for the __2__ of the quotation he was sure it must be. And how he learned, __3__, that it was not a quotation. He also learned that the inscription had been put there by a lonely old __4__ whose pet had been killed by a Nazi bomb.

I always remembered these __5__ words. It's not so much for their poetry and imagery, as for the __6__ they contain. A truth so simple and profound, it seems to me, that it applies to any __7__. For instance, it may be used in the __8__ periods of a great nation, or the small private twilights that come to all of us.

In moments of discouragement or defeat, or even __9__, there are always certain things to cling to. Little things, usually: remembered laughter, the face of a sleeping child, a tree in the wind, in fact any reminder of something deeply felt or __10__ loved. No man is so poor as not to have many of these small candles. And when they are lighted, darkness goes away.

從下列選項中選擇最適當者填入空格中：

(A) lady	(B) situation	(C) dearly	(D) darkest	(E) despair
(F) words	(G) finally	(H) truth	(I) source	(J) inspiring

1. _____ 2. _____ 3. _____ 4. _____ 5. _____

6. _____ 7. _____ 8. _____ 9. _____ 10. _____

gravestone *n.* 墓碑	blitz *v.* 對…猛烈空襲	inscription *n.* 碑文	imagery *n.* 意象
profound *adj.* 深奧的	twilight *n.* 黃昏	cling *v.* 依附	reminder *n.* 提醒物

True Nobility

- -

In a calm sea every man is a pilot.

But all sunshine without shade, all pleasure without pain is not life ___1___. Take the lot of the happiest, ___2___. It is a tangled yarn. Sorrows and blessings, one following another, make us sad and blessed ___3___. Even death itself makes life more ___4___. People come closest to their true selves in the sober moments of life, under the ___5___ of sorrow and loss.

In the affairs of life or of business, it is not intellect that tells so much as character, not brains so much as heart, not genius so much as self-control, patience, and ___6___ regulated by judgment.

I have always believed that the person who has begun to live more ___7___ within begins to live more simply without. In an age of extravagance and waste, I wish I could show to the world how ___8___ the real wants of humanity are.

To regret one's ___9___ to the point of not repeating them is true repentance. There is nothing ___10___ in being superior to some other person. The true nobility is in being superior to your previous self.

從下列選項中選擇最適當者填入空格中：

(A) seriously	(B) at all	(C) noble	(D) errors	(E) for example
(F) by turns	(G) discipline	(H) few	(I) loving	(J) shadows

1. _____	2. _____	3. _____	4. _____	5. _____
6. _____	7. _____	8. _____	9. _____	10. _____

nobility *n.* 高貴	sunshine *n.* 陽光	tangled *adj.* 纏結的	yarn *n.* 紡紗
sober *adj.* 嚴謹的	intellect *n.* 才智	extravagance *n.* 奢侈	repentance *n.* 懺悔

A Better Tomorrow

"I have but one lamp by which my feet are guided, and that is the lamp of experience."
　　　　　　　　　　　　　　　　　　　　　　　　—Patrick Henry

People often ___1___ why historians go to so much trouble to preserve millions of books, documents and records of the past. Why do we have libraries? What ___2___ are these old documents and the history books?

Because sometimes, the voice of experience can cause us to stop, look and ___3___. And because sometimes, past records, correctly interpreted, can give us ___4___ of what to do and what not to do.

If we want to create ___5___ peace, we must seek its origins in human experience. For example, from ___6___ of courageous and devoted people, we got inspirations. In stories of the Christian martyrs, history records the suffering and the heroic deeds of human beings. Surely, these records can ___7___ us in our confusions, and in our yearnings for peace.

The supreme ___8___ of history is a better world. History gives an alert to those who would promote war. History brings inspiration to those who seek peace. History, ___9___, makes us learn. Yesterday's records can ___10___ us from repeating mistakes. And from history, we see the progress of mankind.

從下列選項中選擇最適當者填入空格中：

(A) help	(B) good	(C) lasting	(D) purpose	(E) warning
(F) records	(G) keep	(H) wonder	(I) listen	(J) in short

1. _____　　2. _____　　3. _____　　4. _____　　5. _____

6. _____　　7. _____　　8. _____　　9. _____　　10. _____

martyr *n.* 殉教者　　heroic *adj.* 英勇的　　yearning *n.* 渴望　　supreme *adj.* (重要性) 最高的

Language Note

▶ history *n.* 歷史；歷史學　　　　▶ historian *n.* 歷史學家

▶ historic *adj.* 歷史上有名的、重要的

如：historic sites 史蹟；a historic day 歷史性的日子

▶ historical *adj.* 歷史上的，與歷史有關的

如：a historical novel 歷史小說；historical studies 歷史研究

We Are on a Journey

Wherever you are, and whoever you may be, there is one thing in which you and I are just alike at this moment, and in all the moments of our existence. We are not __1__; we are on a journey. Our life is a movement, a tendency, a steady, ceaseless progress towards an unseen goal. We are gaining something, or __2__ something every day. Even when our position and character seem to remain precisely the same, they are __3__. For the mere advance of time is a change. It is not the same thing to have a bare field in January and in July. The __4__ makes the difference. The behavior that is childlike in the child is __5__ in the man. It is age that tells them apart.

Everything that we do is a step in one __6__ or another. Even the failure to do something is in itself a deed. It sets us forward or __7__. The action of the negative pole of magnetic needle is just as real as the action of the __8__ pole. To __9__ is to accept—the other alternative.

Are you nearer to your port today than yesterday? Yes, you must be a little nearer to some __10__ or other; for since your ship was first launched upon the sea of life, you have never been still for a single moment; the sea is too deep, you could not find an anchorage if you would; there can be no pause until you come into port.

從下列選項中選擇最適當者填入空格中：

| (A) childish | (B) backward | (C) port | (D) at rest | (E) positive |
| (F) decline | (G) changing | (H) losing | (I) direction | (J) season |

1. _____   2. _____   3. _____   4. _____   5. _____

6. _____   7. _____   8. _____   9. _____   10. _____

alternative *n.* 選擇   anchorage *n.* 停泊地

Intermediate Reading:
英文閱讀 *High Five*

王隆興／編著

掌握大考新趨勢，搶先練習新題型！

★ 全書分為5大主題：生態物種、人文歷史、科學科技、環境保育、醫學保健，共50篇由外籍作者精心編寫之文章。

★ 題目仿111學年度學測參考試卷命題方向設計，為未來大考提前作準備，搶先練習第二部分新題型──混合題。

★ 隨書附贈解析夾冊，方便練習後閱讀文章中譯及試題解析，並於解析補充每回文章精選的15個字彙。

修訂三版　108 課綱適用

英語 *Make Me High* 系列

Cloze Test

克漏字與文意選填

解析本

劉美皇 編著

三民書局

克漏字

Unit 1
從食物看個性

　　人們在衣著、汽車、房子上表現出自我的個性。因為我們可能選擇某些食物來向他人「透露」某些與我們有關的事情，所以飲食也能反映出我們的個性。舉例來說，有些人吃的大多為美食，像是魚子醬和龍蝦。此外，他們非在昂貴的餐廳用餐不可 (絕對不在自助餐或是小吃店)，他們或許想「昭告」天下，他們懂得「生活中較為美好的事物」。

　　人類能吃的食物有很多種類，不過素食主義者卻選擇不食用肉類。素食主義者們的共同點不單只在其飲食上，他們的個性也可能很近似。比方說在美國，素食者可能是很有創造力的一群人，他們可能不喜歡競爭強烈的運動或工作，他們擔憂這個世界的安危，且他們很可能對戰爭並不認同。

　　有些人大多吃「速食」。一項研究顯示，許多吃速食的人彼此間有很多共同點。然而，他們跟素食者大不相同，他們喜歡競爭，擅於作生意，而且經常行色匆匆。很多速食者或許不甚同意這個對他們個性的描述，不過這的確是他們的典型寫照。

1. **B** 呼應前半句食物會透露關於我們的事，「我們的飲食也能反映我們的個性」。(A)方言 (C)設計 (D)染料

2. **C** such as... 如…。(A)(B)也就是說 (D)像…，為連接詞，後需接完整子句。such as 的用法見 **Unit 1 Extension**。

3. **D** 由後面括號 「絕不在自助餐館 (cafeteria) 或小吃店 (snack bar) 吃東西」 得知本格選 expensive (貴的)。

4. **A** 「…素食者 (vegetarian) 選擇不吃肉類」。

5. **A** 前句提及他們不僅止於在飲食上有許多共同點，暗示他們在個性上可能也很相似。
(B)不同的 (C)冷漠的 (D)奇怪的

6. **B** worry about... 擔心…。

7. **C** 本句欲表達許多速食者間有許多共同點，用 one another 表「互相」。have a lot in common with... 和…之間有很多共同點。
(A)別人 (B)另一人 (D)每個人

8. **C** A be different from B　A 與 B 不同。

9. **D** be good at... 擅長於…。

10. **D** 「許多速食者或許不同意這個對他們個性的描述」。
(A)處方 (B)訂閱 (C)銘刻；題字

Unit 2
測謊器

　　測謊器是一種設計來顯示一個人是否說實話的機器。在受試者接受質問時，測謊機會測量其身體反應以達成測謊目的。在回答問題時，機器會記錄許多身體上的反應。其所根據的概念在於，當一個人沒說實話，壓力會使身體產生變化。

　　接受測謊器的測驗，需在人體的不同部位安放幾個裝置。胸部和腹部上的膠管用來記錄呼吸；手臂上的裝置用來測量血壓；而身體的反應則由另一個裝置記錄下來。

　　在測謊器測驗的過程當中，首先專家會問一連串的問題。接著，測謊機能顯示一個人據實回答和捏造答案時的身體反應，接著再問到重點問題。整個過程費時約兩個鐘頭，之後再由專家解讀資訊，並判斷出這個人回答問題時是否誠實。

測謊器的應用存有許多爭議，許多人不相信測謊器真的能判別一個人是否說謊。美國測謊器協會表示，在大多時候，一位訓練有素的專家能判斷一個人是否說了謊話。不過就連該協會也坦承，誤判有時會發生。

在美國大多數的法庭，測謊的結果通常無法做為法律上的證據。就美國司法制度能否採用測謊結果一事，其最高法院尚未裁決。然而，該國有些地區已經禁止使用測謊結果當作證據。

1. **B** while 常接進行式表「在⋯期間」，而代名詞 he or she 指被測量的人，句意應為「被質問」，故選(B)。question v. 質問。

2. **A** be based on... 以⋯為依據。
   (B)改為 on the basis of
   (C)改為 according to

3. **C** involve v. 包含。
   (A)使感興趣 (B)介紹 (D)邀請

4. **D** during prep. 在⋯期間，後接名詞。
   (A) while 為連接詞，需接子句

5. **A** 測謊過程中，裝置會顯示一個人據實回答和捏造答案時身體如何反應。

6. **D** sth. take + 時間 某事花費時間。
   (A) (某物) 花費金錢 (B) (某人) 花費金錢 (C) (某人) 花費金錢、時間。
   見 **Unit 8 Extension**。

7. **B** whether 及 if 引導名詞子句，表「是否⋯」。見 **Unit 2 Extension**。

8. **C** lie (說謊) 的過去分詞為 lied。

9. **A** sth. + happen (某事) 發生。
   (D)應刪去 to

10. **A** 否定現在完成式常與 yet 連用，表「尚未⋯」。rule 在本句意指法律上的「裁定」。(B)已經 (C)剛才 (D)自從

安卓克利斯

從前從前，有個奴隸叫做安卓克力斯，他從主人那裡逃跑，躲進森林裡。

在他四處遊走的同時，發現有隻獅子躺在那裡呻吟慘叫。起初他轉身就跑，不過看到獅子沒有追來，他轉過身回到獅子處。走近時，這隻獅子伸出牠的腳掌，整個都腫起來了而且血流不止，安卓克力斯發現有根巨大的刺插在裡頭，這造成獅子的痛苦，他將刺拔出來，並且替獅子的腳掌包紮，不久後獅子已能起身，牠像隻狗一樣舔著安卓克力斯的手。後來獅子把安卓克力斯帶回牠的洞穴，每天都帶肉回來給他吃。

可是不久之後，安卓克力斯和獅子都遭到捕獲，經過判決，要將這個奴隸丟到好幾天都沒有餵食的獅子面前。國王和每位臣子都前來觀看這場好戲，安卓克力斯被領到競技場的中央，稍後獅子也從巢穴中被釋放出來，一面衝向這個犧牲品，一面吼叫。

不過牠一靠近安卓克力斯，就認出這是牠的朋友，牠像隻友善的狗一樣舔著安卓克力斯的手。國王對此十分吃驚，就把他叫來面前，於是安卓克力斯將事情的經過告訴了他，聽了之後，國王赦免且釋放了這名奴隸，也將獅子放回森林裡。

感恩是高貴靈魂的表徵。

1. **D** find + O. + O.C. 發現某人 (物)⋯。因受詞 lion 和其補語 lie down (躺臥) 間為主動關係，選現在分詞片語 lying down。lie (躺) 的動詞三態為 lie-lay-lain，現在分詞為 lying。

2. **A** 本格後說他轉身跑開，而後半句說他又轉身回來，可知此處選 at first (起初)。

(B)最後 (C)至少 (D)逍遙法外的

3. **B** 由本句前半所提獅子的腳掌腫脹 (swollen) 且流血 (bleeding)，可知這根刺造成獅子的痛苦。

4. **A** bind up 包紮。
   (B)(C)綁在… (D)用…捆綁

5. **C** bring sb. sth. 將某物帶來給某人，詳見 **Unit 3 Extension**。
   (A)改為 ...provided him with meat...
   (B) take sb. sth. 將某物帶去他處給某人，語意錯誤 (D) carry 後面接 sth.

6. **B** 奴隸被丟到已有好幾天沒被餵食的獅子前。用過去完成式表示在過去一個動作發生前已持續一段時間的另一動作。

7. **A** 分詞結構的 bounding and roaring 與 the lion 為主動關係，表附帶狀況，句意為「一面衝向受害者，一面吼叫」。

8. **C** 由後文「…像隻友善的狗般舔他的手」，可知獅子認出牠的朋友了。
   (A)拒絕 (B)記錄 (D)報告

9. **D** be surprised/amazed at... 對…感到吃驚。

10. **A** 「…國王赦免 (pardon) 並釋放了奴隸…」。(B)返回 (C)提醒 (D)使 (痛苦) 和緩

Unit 4
網路禮節——你不可不知的守則

維吉尼亞·席亞 (Virginia Shea) 在著作《網路禮節》中列了一張表，舉出在網路世界中與人恰當溝通所應遵行的「要」與「不要」，以下是她的幾點建議。

第一，切記你的訊息是發給一個活生生的人，而不只是一臺電腦，不要打一些你平常不會當著別人的面說的話，另外也要記得，收到訊息的人沒辦法聽見你說話的語氣，也看不見你臉上的表情，所以務必把意思表達清楚。

不要在線上做些你在現實生活中不會做的事。除非是免費的東西，否則不要沒付費就任意拿取。不要偷看別人的電子郵件——你總不會打開鄰居的信箱，然後拆開他們的信吧？倒是要多和人分享網路上的知識，這裡是個充斥著大量資訊的大型空間，有許多新鮮事等著 (你) 去發現。

要記得別人是以你的文章和行動來評斷你這個人，所以務必善加書寫。良好的寫作技巧以及正確的文法與拼字十分重要。若不確定某個字怎麼拼或者該用哪個片語，一定要查閱它，有不少有用的書籍和網站可以幫助你。

可以在網路上某些討論區表達自己的意見，例如聊天室或留言板，但別和他人起了爭執，線上文字戰爭的討論串讀起來或許有趣，但通常對網路群組的其他成員來說並不公平。

在網路上就跟在現實生活中一樣，要多尊重他人的空間、隱私及感受。要謹記，在這條資訊高速公路上來來去去的不是只有你而已！

1. **C** 本句為倒裝句，主詞是複數的 some of her suggestions，故選(C)複數的 be 動詞。見 **Unit 4 Extension**。

2. **A** expression *n.* 表情。
   (B)印象 (C)憂鬱 (D)壓迫

3. **B** 因為在網路上無法聽到聲音或看到表情，所以要確認你的意思是清楚的。(A)乾淨的 (C)模糊的 (D)模稜兩可的

4. **D** 「不可沒付錢就拿走東西，除非它是免費的。」

5. **D** 由前後可知本格需填介系詞，用 with 表「有著…」。with 的用法見 **Unit 10 Extension**。(B)本句已有動詞，句法錯誤 (C)應改為 that has

6. **A** A as well B... 不僅 B 而且 A，因重點在於 A，所以動詞與 A 一致，本句動詞與 good writing skills 一致，見 **Unit 5 Extension**。matter *v.* 重要，前用助動詞 do 強調語氣。

7. **B** look up... 查閱…。(D)為它送行

8. **B** like *prep.* 像是。(A) as 為連接詞，接子句 (C)應改為 such as (D)包括，句法錯誤

9. **C** 本句主詞 flame wars 為複數，需接複數 be 動詞 are。flame 原意為「火焰」，在網路用語則有「火藥味的電郵或網路訊息」的意思，這裡的 "flame wars" 意指充滿火藥味一連串相互攻擊的網路文字。

10. **D** try to + V 努力、設法做…，句意為「設法尊重他人的空間…」。(A)(B) remain 為不及物動詞，後不可接受詞 (C) try + V-ing 試試看會有什麼結果

Unit 5
美國人對工作的態度

對大多數的美國人來說，工作十分重要。一份工作不僅提供薪水，也給他們一種認同感。美國人剛認識別人時，通常問的第一個問題就是：「你在哪高就？」

對大多的美國人來說，工作很重要；換句話說，他們認為工作比絕大多數的事情都來得重要，是要擺在第一位的。他們可能不是樂於工作，但他們仍然認為「工作重於玩樂」，或「正事比享樂重要」。美國學生通常對於課業的態度也是如此。舉

例來說，美國的高中生或大學生若在上課途中巧遇友人，通常會跟朋友打聲招呼，寒暄幾句，然後就說：「我得走了，我還有課。」這樣一點也不失禮。要是朋友想要來拜訪，他們會相約課後的其他時間見面。

美國人不希望朋友改變他的工作行程表只為了聚在一起碰面－不管是預先計劃好的或是突然的拜訪都是如此。朋友會規劃時間在彼此都沒有工作時見上一面，為了聚在一起而希望朋友工作遲到、上課遲到，或是錯失一天的工作，是很失禮的。這在商業界中尤其如此，身在其中最重要的就是顯出責任感。

但很值得注意的是，工作排在優先的位置並不代表對美國人來說，工作比友情重要。這不過表示從時間和計畫表來說，工作通常比其他事物優先。

1. **C** not only A but also B... 不僅 A 而且 B…。「一份工作不僅提供他們薪水 (paycheck)，也給他們一種認同感 (a sense of identity)」。見 **Unit 5 Extension**。

2. **A** 本格前提到對大多數美國人來說，工作是很重要，後則進一步解釋它，故選 that is (也就是說)。

3. **D** 本格前提到美國人也許不樂於工作，後談到他們仍然認為工作重於玩樂，前後語意相對，故選對等連接詞 but。

4. **A** run into... 巧遇…。
   (B)想到 (C)調查 (D)闖入

5. **C** arrange to + V 安排做…。

6. **C** either A or B 不是 A 就是 B。見 **Unit 5 Extension**。
   accidental *adj.* 意外的。

7. **D** 「…當兩者皆不在工作時」。
   neither *adj.* (兩者中) 任一皆不。

8. **B** be late for + N 遲到。

　　(C)後面須接動詞

9. **C** where/in which 連接形容詞子句去修飾表場所的先行詞 the business world，見 **Unit 19 Extension**。where/in which 前有逗點，為非限定用法。essential *adj.* 必要的。

10. **A** priority *n.* 優先考慮的事。

　　(B)品質　(C)數量　(D)個性

Unit 6
大象

　　大象是世界上最大的陸生哺乳動物，牠們居住於兩大洲——非洲和南亞洲。亞洲象，又以印度象為人所知，比非洲象容易馴服，你在馬戲團和動物園看到的象幾乎總是亞洲象。非洲象較大，有著扇子般的大耳。非洲象和印度象都有強壯堅硬的皮膚和迷人的長牙，那成了牠們的問題。象目前處在危機中，人們為了使用牠們的皮和長牙而殺害這些動物。恐怕到了本世紀末，這些大型的哺乳動物就會絕種。然而，大象在非洲部分地區卻是問題所在。在這群最大型動物聚集的地區，對農夫而言牠們成了巨大的有害動物。沒有籬笆堅固到能使這些龐然大物遠離農作物。大象想去哪就去哪，破壞食用作物和農舍。非洲農夫不知道他們是否能允許大象在他們鄰近的地方繼續生存。

　　十年前，在非洲有一百三十多萬頭大象。過去十年間，該數量已經減少到大約 60 萬。為了高價的象牙，非洲象被獵殺。大部分是被盜獵者獵殺，盜獵者就是非法殺害動物的獵人。成年的大象每天吃多達 300 磅重的食物，當牠們找食物的時候，時常走到很遠的地方。當牠們無法找到牠們喜歡吃的草時，牠們會將樹木從地上拔

起。

　　今日象群居住的地區遠比從前要小。許多牠們路徑通過的地區已經變成農場。而有些大象因為踐踏農夫的農作物被農夫殺害。

　　我們的政府已經通過保護大象的法規。人們不准進口或攜入象牙製品或大象身體的任何部分。此外，我們必須透過教育，推廣保育大象的重要性。

1. **B** be known as... 以…身分為人所知。

　　(A)因…有名　(C)(D)句意為被動，不可用現在分詞

2. **B** in danger 身陷危險。

　　(A)有危險性的　(C)危害　(D)脫險

3. **A** 前句提及大象有絕種 (extinct) 之虞，後面談到大象同時也在部分地區製造問題，用 however (然而) 表語氣轉折。

4. **C** 逗點前是完整句，後為表「連續或附帶狀況的」分詞構句形式。主詞 elephant 和 destroy 之間為主動關係，故選 destroying。

5. **D** wonder if/whether... 不確定是否…。if 引導名詞子句，見 **Unit 2 Extension**。

6. **A** 用現在完成式表示「已經…」，句意為「…數量已經減少到…」。

7. **C** as much as... 和…一樣多，用於肯定句。(A)(B)用於否定句

8. **D** strip sb./sth. of 奪取某人 (物) 的…。詳見 **Unit 6 Extension**。

9. **A** in which elephant herds live 為關係子句修飾先行詞 the area，見 **Unit 19 Extension**。herd *n.* (牛、馬等) 群。(B)介系詞後的關係代名詞不可用 that　(C) where 是關係副詞不用加 in　(D) there 非關係代名詞

10. **B** 本句可還原為 ...items (which/that are) made from ivory or any part of the elephant's body. be made from... 由…製成。ivory *n.* 象牙。

Unit 7
洞穴裡的住家

　　你聽過最特別的房子是哪一種？我們都知道人類在很久以前是住在洞穴裡，不過你可曾知道，現今西班牙南部有數以千計的人住在洞穴中的住家？在土耳其中部，你可以看到一整個村莊都是洞穴的房子，其中有些已經歷時將近兩千年；而在中國的長江附近,也有數百萬的人住在洞穴屋。

　　住在這些房子裡比你想像要來得舒適，它們很自然就是冬暖夏涼，地板上通常鋪上瓷磚或地毯，牆壁經過粉刷，也有門和窗戶。許多穴居的住家都有電話，有的甚至還有傳真和網路連結。在西班牙的瓜地克斯 (Guadix)，你可以眺望表層布滿了底下洞穴屋所裝設的電視電線的小山坡。

　　在特魯 (Troo) 村也許可以找到世界上最豪華摩登的穴居住宅，這是位於法國羅亞爾河谷地的一個村莊。數百年來，該地區的洞穴一直用來儲存酒類和栽種蘑菇，近年來，這些洞穴都裝配了現代化便利設施，像是自來水和電力，甚至還有一處餐廳可以供應五道菜餚的餐點。如今有不少富有的巴黎人用這些洞穴當另一個家,因為這些洞穴有別於城市的快速步調，提供了一個涼爽、輕鬆的環境轉換。

　　要是到這些地方的某些地點去旅行，你甚至能找到位於洞穴的旅館。例如在土耳其卡帕多奇亞 (Cappadocia) 的一個村落中,你可以投宿一間由石灰岩所雕鑿出來的房子，裡頭有十一個房間，每一間都有各自的衛浴和電話，而雙人房每晚的價錢大約是五十美元。你可以獲得居住在洞穴中一、兩個晚上的獨特經驗。

1. **C** 前後兩個子句間沒有連接詞，應填兼具代名詞及連接詞功能的關係代名詞 which。(A)本句需改為 and some of them... (D) that 不用於非限定用法的關係子句

2. **B** 本句主詞為動名詞片語，因後接形容詞，選單數 be 動詞 is。見 **Unit 7 Extension**。

3. **D** 由前句 comfortable，可推知這些房子夏天涼爽 (cool) 冬天溫暖 (warm)。

4. **A** 本格後「有傳真和網路連結」更勝於前半句「有電話」，故選 even (甚至)。

5. **A** be situated in... 位於…。本句可還原為：...the village of Troo, (which is) situated in...。(B)應改為 located

6. **B** be fitted with... 被安裝…。(A)被變成… (C)被…覆蓋 (D)應改為 equipped with

7. **C** 「數字＋單數單位名詞」構成複合形容詞，故選 5-course (五道菜的)。見 **Unit 11 Extension**。

8. **D** 相對於洞穴的輕鬆 (relaxing)、涼爽，可知此處為城市的快步調。

9. **A** 本句舉例說明前句所提的洞穴中的旅館，故選 for example (例如)。(B)實際上 (C)此外 (D)也就是說

10. **B** sth. cost ＋ 金錢 某物花費金錢，見 **Unit 8 Extension**。(A)花費，主詞需為人 (C)損失 (D)浪費

Unit 8
樂透贏家——富有，但快樂嗎？

　　每週購買彩券和贏得彩券的金額有上

百萬美元，許多彩券的頭獎獎金更可高達一億美元，而彩券得主發現他們突然有了從未擁有過的大筆金錢。很多得主的錢足以買輛新車、蓋棟豪宅、去渡個假，並且將工作辭掉，這一切都發生在短短的時間之內。不過，這些少數幸運贏得頭彩的人，也可能以更多的問題收場。

彩券的發行機構聘請諮詢人員來幫助頭彩得主，這些諮詢人員鼓勵彩金得主向理財專家，比如說會計師，徵詢該怎樣投資這筆錢會最好的意見，這些諮詢人員也會幫助得主了解，怎樣可以讓他們的生活變得更好，怎樣可能變得更糟。好在許多的頭彩得主都能將財富運用得宜，不過有些得主卻沒能明智地運用這筆錢，因而落得負債的下場，連求個收支平衡都成問題。

很多樂透得主所犯的最大錯誤就是過度揮霍。有個服務生贏得了加州的樂透後，兩百萬美元的獎金全數用來購物、開派對、借錢給朋友，中獎後短短幾個月就破產了，只好再去當售貨員。

不管獎金有多少，若彩券得主過度揮霍又沒有聰明投資，錢總有花完的危險。彩券得主也應該要記得，他們贏得的錢當中要支付一大筆稅金給政府。因此，即使一夕致富，他們仍須審慎規劃每一筆開銷。

1. **A** as much as... 多達⋯⋯，用於不可數名詞。(B)用於可數名詞 (C)(D)用於否定句

2. **B** quit/stop + V-ing 停止做⋯⋯，quit working 表「停止工作」。(A) stop to + V 停下某事去做⋯⋯，句意不合。

3. **C** 前面提及贏得彩券的種種好處，本句談到彩券得主可能遇到更多問題，用 however (然而) 表語氣的轉折。(A)所以 (B)此外 (D)起先

4. **B** 由 encourage sb. + to V (鼓勵某人

做⋯) 的句型可知本格填不定詞片語。get advice 徵詢意見。learn a lesson 學到教訓。

5. **D** 「⋯他們的生活可以變得更好，也可能變得更壞」。

6. **A** 本格前指出有些得獎者沒有明智地運用金錢，後面提及他們的下場，故選 as a result (結果)。
   (B)事實上 (C)相反地 (D)除此之外

7. **C** spend + 金錢 + (in) V-ing 在⋯事上花費金錢，見 **Unit 8 Extension**。依句意選 lending (借出)。(A)(B)借入

8. **A** broke *adj.* 破產的。(B)破碎的 (C)破產，為名詞，應改為 bankrupt

9. **B** no matter how... 無論如何⋯⋯。
   (C)縱然 (D)無論何事

10. **A** winnings *n.* 獎金，可數名詞，故選
    (A)大量的 (B)應改為 a large quantity of (C)一大塊 (片) (D)只可接不可數名詞

Unit 9
旅遊方式大不同

人們在家中的生活方式有所不同，「在路上」的生活方式也是大異其趣。有些旅行者偏好住大型的旅館，在高價的餐廳用餐，並把注意力集中在最著名的旅遊景點；而有些人認為觀光只是旅行的原因之一，而非唯一的原因。他們想要認識各式各樣的人，了解不同的意見、價值觀以及問題，為此，他們在平價的旅館中或在露營區等地方認識其他的旅行者。此外，他們也對餐廳、公園、購物中心、遊樂區等處的人們細心觀察，藉此設法認識新的地方。

另外，還有些旅行者喜歡藉著和所造訪之處的當地人相處，來了解當地的文化。有少部分的人甚至待在當地的私人家庭

中。這是怎麼辦到的呢？對於有心體驗不同於自身生活方式的人，不少國際組織提供了具教育意義的體驗，藉由 American Field Service、the Experiment in International Living 等行程，以及交換旅遊、語言課程等計畫，遊客可以體驗其他地方的生活。參與這些活動的人通常是學生，可以在為期數週、數月、甚至長達一年的寄宿家庭期間，認識當地的人。

當然不是每個旅行者都有很多時間可以長期待在寄宿家庭，不過，只有短暫假期的觀光客還是有機會與某個地區的當地人進行資訊與意見的交流。這些提供此類機會的機構中，有一個名為 Servas International。它數年來撮合了國家、宗教、文化、財經背景各異的人，該團體讓旅行者有機會認識世界各地的人。

1. **D** 投宿旅館為短暫停留，故用 stay v. 暫住。prefer 的用法見 **Unit 9 Extension**。

2. **A** 本格與前一句形成 Some...others... (有些是…有些則…) 的句型。

3. **D** 承接上一句談到他們如何認識其他的旅行者，本格選 moreover (此外)，進一步地陳述他們如何認識新的地方。(A)然而 (B)反而 (C)因此

4. **A** 本句陳述與前段兩種類型不同的旅行者，故選 still (還有，另外)。

5. **B** 形容詞子句 which is different from 省略 which is，修飾前面的先行詞 lifestyles。(C)與…相同 (D)與…相似

6. **B** such as... 如…，見 **Unit 1 Extension**。(A)不但…並且… (C)包括，為動詞 (D)有別於…

7. **C** even adv. 甚至，加強語氣強調一年的長度。(A)曾經 (B)只有 (D)結構不對

8. **C** 本格前提到並非每位旅行者都有很

多時間，而本格後談到他們還是有機會，依語氣應選 nevertheless (儘管如此)。(A)例如 (B)結果 (D)相反地

9. **D** 本格依文意判斷，應使用被動語態，故選(D)。

10. **B** 本句為現在完成進行式，用 for 後接一段時間 many years 表「數年來」，從過去持續至今且繼續進行中。(A)在某個期間內，不用於現在完成式 (C)從…以來，後接事件發生的時間點 (D)到 (至某個時間點為止)

Unit 10
紐西蘭

紐西蘭是由兩個主要的島嶼所組成，一為北島，另一為南島，前者的特色就是火山綿延，而後者天氣較為嚴寒，有著滿布霜雪、冰河的高山景色，南、北兩島都有很多的淡水湖泊，也有不少河川流向太平洋。

由於紐西蘭在海中孤立，所以有很多動植物是世界上其他地方看不到的，最為人所熟知的動物要算是象徵該國，且很受歡迎的鷸鴕了，這種鳥類是夜行性動物，不會飛；紐西蘭還是考里松的故鄉，這種樹高達三十公尺，壽命可達兩千年之久。紐西蘭大多國土都在國家公園的範圍內，森林和野生生物都受其良好的保護。

最早住在紐西蘭的是毛利人，一千年前，他們從附近的小島遷徙過來。兩個世紀前，英國人率領歐洲人前來建立殖民地。而今，毛利文化歷久不衰，和其他世界各地來到紐西蘭定居的人帶來的文化充分融合。紐西蘭人口大約四百萬人，大多數的人都住在北島。

紐西蘭以愛好自然者的樂園為人所

知，同時也是戶外活動的絕佳場所，登山健行或是滑雪都很適合，而當地生活進步，人民生性友善，更使得紐西蘭成為旅遊觀光的絕佳去處。

1. **C** one...the other... (兩者當中) 其一…另一。

2. **A** a series of... 一連串的…。volcano *n.* 火山。(B)一群 (鳥) (C)一群 (魚) (D)一大筆 (錢)

3. **C** 「那裡有」 在英文中用 there + be 表示，配合後方名詞為複數，故選 (C) are。

4. **B** 助動詞 can 在主詞 so many... animals 前，可推知句首為以 nowhere 起首的否定副詞片語，構成否定倒裝句，句意為「世界上其他地方無法…」。見 **Unit 4 Extension**。

5. **B** 本格後接一段時間，故選 as long as (長達…)。
   (A)遠及… (C)一…就 (D)如…年長

6. **D** 本句可還原為 ...Europeans (who were) led by the British... ，省略了 who were ，以過去分詞片語修飾 Europeans。

7. **A** remain 為連綴動詞，後接形容詞當主詞補語，表「保持…的狀態」。
   (C) remain 後亦可接名詞當主詞補語，但表「保持…身分」，語意錯誤

8. **C** with 引導表附帶情況的片語。見 **Unit 10 Extension**。

9. **B** be known as... 以…身份為人所知。

10. **C** 本格為形容詞子句 who enjoy 省略 who，動詞依主動語態改為 V-ing。

Unit 11
東方的召喚

　　彭蒙惠出生於美國西雅圖的一個基督教家庭，家中有八個兄弟姊妹。在她十一歲參加的夏令營活動中，有位來自中國的牧師談起他古老的國家，一聽到他的演說，彭蒙惠便立志長大以後要去中國傳道。

　　一九四八年，二十一歲的彭蒙惠放棄了紐約伊士曼音樂學院的獎學金，與成為一個小喇叭演奏家的夢想，反而選擇成為一個傳教士，搭了六個禮拜的船到中國。途經東京、釜山、馬尼拉、香港，來到戰亂的上海。國共內戰迫使她一路逃難到重慶、蘭州、香港，最後才隨教會來到臺灣。

　　彭蒙惠踏上臺灣土地後，注意到東岸人煙稀少，很多地方還沒有教會，於是決定在花蓮展開她的傳教工作。

　　一九五一年，她進入花蓮玉山神學院教音樂，並且負責訓練主日學老師。不久她成立了一個小小的教會，以及一個小小的主日學班級。她開始教導主日學的學生們基督教信仰，同時自己也學會一些當地原住民的語言。每當小朋友邀她到家裡，儘管怪腔怪調，她總是用她才剛學會的語言跟他們溝通。那些家庭聽到她用他們的語言打招呼，一開始覺得很奇怪，但最後都因她的努力而笑開了嘴。

1. **B** where/at which 連接形容詞子句，修飾表場所的先行詞 a summer camp。見 **Unit 19 Extension**。

2. **C** on/upon + V-ing 一…就…。(A)改為 When 或本句改為 When she heard (B)自從，用於現在完成式 (D)改為 Because of

3. **A** give up... 放棄…。由後面一句反而選擇成為… (Choosing instead to be...) 得知此處語意為「放棄」原有

夢想。(B)拒絕 (C)建立 (D)實現

4. **D** week 為時間單位，與數字構成複合形容詞時，需用單數。見 **Unit 11 Extension**。

5. **D** force sb. to + V 強迫某人做…。亦可用 force sb. into + V-ing。

6. **A** set up... 創立…，開辦…。
   (B)起床 (C)以…結束 (D)彌補；捏造

7. **B** establish v. 建立，成立。
   (A)出版 (C)達成 (D)廢止

8. **B** pick up... (片段性地) 學習…。對等連接詞 and 連接本格與前面的 taught，故應填過去式動詞。
   (C)(D)用盡…

9. **C** in spite of... 儘管…。「…她總是使用她才剛學會的語言，儘管怪腔怪調」。(A)代替 (B)害怕 (D)除了

10. **C** 感官動詞 hear，其後的受詞與動詞 greet (打招呼) 間為主動關係，用原形動詞。

Unit 12
正式書信是垂死的藝術嗎？

不用說，網際網路的快速方便已經大大地改變了我們的生活。現在，比起使用郵政系統的信件寄送 (現在常被稱為 「龜速郵件」)，發送電子郵件成了多數人較為偏愛的溝通方式。

在一項由電子郵件服務提供者 MSN Hotmail 針對兩千名年輕人所進行的調查中，約有半數人表示他們是以電子郵件發送感謝函，而非以郵寄的方式。除了發送較為私人的電子郵件外，時下投入職場的年輕人發現，自己每週要發送、回覆數百封的商業電子郵件。

然而，同一批年輕人中，很多似乎都沒注意到工作時發送電子郵件的一些基本規則。大多數回答問卷的人表示，在按下「傳送」鍵之前，不會檢查他們的拼字或標點，更令人吃驚的是，每二十位應答者中就有一位表示，他們有時在給上司的信件中，是以「愛你唷！(love and kisses!)」結尾，這一般在職場中可是被視為有失禮節的。

會在工作場合的電子郵件中用這種非正式的語法，主要原因在於多數年輕人一直以來都是在網際網路，以輕鬆親切的方式和他人溝通，其中又以使用社群網站為然。對很多人來說，下班之後網路上的溝通不外乎與其他人在聊天室中閒談，在留言板上張貼文章，以及發送電子郵件給朋友。這些一切都是只是好玩而已。

跟以前比起來，愈來愈多的商業書信往來是透過網際網路，因此特別是在使用電子郵件時，知道私人和商業溝通間語言使用上的不同之處是很重要的。人們應該永遠記住，處理商務電子郵件時要保持禮貌。

1. **D** A rather than B... A 而非 B…，動詞與 A 一致。見 **Unit 5 Extension**。語意為「發送電子郵件——而非使用郵政系統寄送信件…」。postal n. 郵政的。

2. **B** 本句可還原成 In a survey...(which was) conducted by... ，省略了 which was，用過去分詞片語修飾 survey。conduct a survey 進行調查。

3. **C** in addition to... 除…之外。其後接名詞或動名詞。見 **Unit 12 Extension**。
   (A)儘管 (B)因為 (C)為了

4. **A** when it comes to + N 提及…時。本格動詞需加 ing 字尾成為動名詞，故選(A) sending。
   (C)收到，與下文不合

5. **A** 本格為形容詞子句 who responded 省略 who，動詞依主動語態改為 V-ing。

6. **A** 本句為倒裝句，句型為主詞補語 + be + 主詞，以 that 引導結構完整的名詞子句作主詞。倒裝句句型見 **Unit 4 Extension**。

7. **B** informal *adj.* 不正式的。
   (A)重要的 (C)不朽的 (D)不便的

8. **C** involve *v.* 包含。(A)包括，需加 "s" (B)排除 (D)本格需填動詞

9. **D** for fun 為了好玩。
   (A)徒勞無功 (B)故意 (C)因公事

10. **D** be aware of... 知道⋯。

Unit 13
電子競技算是體育項目嗎？

　　人就愛競爭，古往今來發生過許多這種例子。比賽的意義是測試參賽者的技巧和實力。人們常常在運動賽事中彼此較勁，希望能奪冠。這些賽事大受歡迎，以致於最後發展出奧運這樣的大型活動。想要參與運動賽事、以及觀眾想要觀賽的渴望，一直都是人類歷史的一部分。

　　時至今日，科技重新界定了運動賽事的意義。在電玩世界，現在有職業「運動選手」，會互相比試，且吸引到大批想觀賞他們身手的觀眾。這些選手能自行出賽，或組團參賽，就像奧運比賽一樣。然而，這些玩家不必接受嚴格的體能訓練以便備戰，而是盯著螢幕磨練技能。

　　那些功力達到頂級、進入電玩大賽的人是職業的。基本上，這代表有足夠的獎金能讓玩家贏取來維持生計。在臺灣，這些玩家通常會加入臺灣電子競技聯盟。

　　臺灣電子競技聯盟成立於二〇〇八年，將電競比賽搬上電視螢幕。那些玩家支領底薪，一起入住團隊宿舍裡。就像運動員，他們有贏得比賽的內驅力。

　　儘管電競很受歡迎，臺灣政府仍未承認它是正式運動項目。反對意見之一是，電競非奧運項目，故不該被視為運動產業的一環。然而，其他國家已認可電競為正式運動，臺灣政府也有部分官員支持給予官方認可。但電競的未來如何還很難說。

1. **B** 這裡是由關係子句所簡化而成的分詞片語，用來修飾前面的名詞 those。原句為 "...those who play them."，因為 play 是主動進行的動作，因此在把關係子句中的主詞省略後，play 要改為 playing。

2. **C** compete against... 與⋯競爭。

3. **A** 由於在第二個空格後面是完整的子句，從句子結構可以判斷應該是指「如此⋯以致於⋯」的句型，但因為空格中間是形容詞 popular，所以必須使用 so...that，而不能使用 such...that，因為 such...that... 的中間要放名詞或名詞片語。

4. **A** 由句子結構判斷，空格後面應該是關係子句，而先行詞 "athletes" 是「運動員」，故關代要選擇 who。

5. **D** 由文意判斷，此處是指「不是⋯而是⋯」的意思，故要選擇 rather than。(A)(B)由於⋯ (C)根據

6. **C** 由文意判斷，此處是指「有足夠的獎金讓選手們去獲得，好讓他們能夠以此賺錢謀生」，故要選 make a living。(A)熬夜 (B)拖延 (D)偶然碰上

7. **B** 由句型判斷，此處應是「分詞構句」的句型，而主要子句的主詞是 TeSL 這個組織，因此可以判斷該組織是「被成立的」，答案要選擇表示被動的過去分詞 Founded。

8. **D** 由於前後句子有「對比」的意味，因此可判斷應該使用表示「雖然、儘管」的介系詞 despite。

9. **D** 此處的句型是 A be considered (to be) B 的句型，表示「A 被認為是 B」。關於本用法的說明，請見 **Unit 13 Extension**。

10. **A** 本句意為「然而，其他國家已經承認電子競技為合法的運動…」。
(B)古典的 (C)最初的 (D)頻繁的

Unit 14
鮭魚

大西洋鮭魚是在注入大西洋的淡水河川中孵化的。鮭魚待在淡水的河川整整兩年，不斷成長至九英寸左右為止，然後牠們就開始游向河川下游。游往河川下游是趟艱辛的旅途，到達海洋之前，很多未成熟的鮭魚遭到包括人類和熊等掠食者的捕捉。在旅途中存活下來並成功抵達大西洋的鮭魚游到很遠的地方，直到格陵蘭島附近的淺灘，接下來的兩、三年就在該地區成長，有時可重達二十磅，甚至更重。

四、五歲時，鮭魚會返回牠們原本的孵化地去產卵，科學家無法解釋鮭魚為什麼會回去，也無法解釋為什麼所有的鮭魚都同時回去，事實上，沒有人知道鮭魚是如何辦到的。除非鮭魚被漁夫或其他掠食者捕捉，否則牠們能游回河的源頭，產卵後再回到海中。

儘管鮭魚一直受到本能以及自身「勇氣」的驅使，但這種週期很容易就遭到破壞。舉例來說，在十九世紀初，康乃狄克河有很多這種魚，但最後一隻於一八七四年遭人捕捉。人類所創造的現代世界，破壞了鮭魚的環境，建造發電的水庫，擾亂了魚群且妨礙了牠們游回到上游的產卵

地，而工廠將污染物及高溫的廢水排放到康乃狄克河，造成河川不適合魚類生存。大西洋鮭魚從康乃狄克河消失了，而新英格蘭地區絕大多數的水域也無法見到牠們的蹤影了。

1. **B** inch (英寸) 是長度單位，故選(B)。
(A)用於年齡 (C)用於高度 (D)用於深度

2. **C** reach v. 抵達。副詞子句原為 "before they reach..."，因與前主要子句的主詞一致，可改為 "before reaching..." 的分詞構句型式，見 **Unit 18 Extension**。(A)改為 they arrive at (B)改為 they reach (D)與…合得來

3. **C** 本格引導一個非限定的關係子句，修飾地點格陵蘭島 (the island of Greenland)，需以 in which 或關係副詞 where 連接。

4. **A** nor 為連接詞，用於否定句後，表「也不…」，後需倒裝。見 **Unit 14 Extension**。

5. **D** 本格前句敘述科學家無法解釋鮭魚的行為，後面談到沒有人知道鮭魚如何辦到，用 in fact (事實上) 進一步陳述前述事實。
(A)總之 (B)事先 (C)結果

6. **A** salmon 單複數同形，由後半句 "they swim to..." 可判斷 salmon 在這裡為複數，後接複數動詞 are。(C)(D)被養育。見 **Unit 14 Extension**

7. **B** 前句提及鮭魚的這種週期易受破壞 (fragile)，本句舉出在康乃狄克河發生的例子，故選 for instance (例如)。
(A) (理由) 其一為… (C)永久地
(D)一定

8. **D** 「人類所創造的現代化世界破壞

(destroy) 了鮭魚的環境」。

9. **A** keep...from + V-ing 使…無法…。

10. **B** pollution *n.* 污染物。

　　(A)人口　(C)比例　(D)財產

Unit 15
挑戰你身體的極限

　　運動員藉由不斷嘗試在他們選擇的運動項目中，比過去其他的運動員更快、更高、更遠，將自己身心的耐力推到極限。這麼做的時候，不少運動員冒著受傷的風險，而許多運動員花了幾個禮拜甚至幾個月的時間，才從訓練時身體所受的傷害中復原。

　　全世界最傑出的運動員每四年齊聚於奧林匹克運動會，在此一盛會，他們展現其運動的技巧與能力，二〇〇〇年雪黎奧運會時，英國有位名為史蒂夫·雷德格瑞夫 (Steve Redgrave) 的運動員，向全世界展示了人體身心的能耐。雷德格瑞夫不僅得過九面世界錦標賽的金牌，還曾於一九八四、一九八八、一九九二、一九九六年贏得奧運划船項目的金牌，他是該項運動中最頂尖的運動員之一。

　　在雪黎奧運前的長期訓練期間，史蒂夫的健康出了許多問題。一九九七年他因為盲腸炎而開刀，一九九八年又診斷出患有糖尿病，這等於說他每天都要注射胰島素，才能控制自己的血糖。不過雷德格瑞夫並未就此放棄划船這項十分耗費體力的運動，他還是選擇繼續進行奧運所需的累人訓練。即使身體出了問題，他仍然不想放棄。

　　在雪黎奧運，史蒂夫和他的隊友划向勝利，贏得第五面奧運金牌。雷德格瑞夫非凡的成就，向世人證明了決心能幫助一個人對付疾病、克服疾病。時至今日，他

仍是唯一曾在耐力型運動項目贏得五屆奧運金牌的人。

1. **A** risk + N/V-ing 冒…的危險。本格後接受詞 themselves，故選動名詞 injuring。athlete *n.* 運動員。

2. **B** do/cause damage to... 對…造成傷害。

3. **A** every four years 表示「每四年一次」。見 **Unit 15 Extension**。

4. **C** 因本格後的子句缺一受詞，故選複合關係代名詞 what。見 **Unit 15 Extension**。

5. **A** as well as 也。

　　(B)除了…之外　(C)只要　(D)期望

6. **D** lead up to... 漸漸接近…。

　　本句可還原為：...long training periods that lead up to (=leading up to) the Sydney Olympics.

7. **B** help sb. (to) + V 幫助某人做…，故選原形動詞 control。(D) help sb. with + N 幫助某人…，with 需接名詞

8. **C** 相對於前半句放棄划船 (rowing)，後半句他選擇繼續進行訓練，用 instead of (反而…) 表前後語意相對。(A)不管　(B)除了…之外　(D)倘若

9. **D** 「即使他的身體有病，他仍然不想放棄。」

　　(A)直到　(B)彷彿　(C)只在…的時候

10. **B** overcome *v.* 克服。

　　(A)因 (疾病) 受苦　(C)贏得　(D)忽略

Unit 16
亞馬遜雨林

　　位於南美洲的亞馬遜雨林，是全世界最廣大的雨林，綿延橫跨九個國家，涵蓋的面積等於半個歐洲的大小。它不僅包含源遠流長的亞馬遜河，還有數百萬種的昆

蟲、鳥類、動植物、樹木等。

　　亞馬遜雨林極其廣闊，以至於對全球的氣候型態有直接影響。雨林作為地球之肺，製造大量供人類與動物呼吸所需的氧氣；雨林也因維持大氣的平衡，而能防止全球暖化現象。基於這些理由，雨林的價值不能用金錢的角度來衡量，但不幸地，實際上這卻是現行的方式。

　　極多可用來生產硬木材的樹種都已砍伐殆盡，銷售到國際市場上，幾個雨林的區域已慘遭焚燬，取而代之的是外來樹種。這些新栽種的樹木被用來製造橡膠和紙張。還有些地方只為了提供農夫們更多田野放牧牛隻而被燒燬。一旦雨林被如此破壞，土壤就會嚴重受損，土地開始被侵蝕。

　　各地的人都對亞馬遜雨林的破壞感到擔憂。儘管對於這個問題有著高度意識，但為了自身的商業利益，人們仍持續地破壞雨林。然而，的確在現實面上，雨林富含太多的資源，以致於難以期望人們與公司商號放手。我們只能希望，當雨林的資源被使用時，是以一種不會對全世界最珍貴資產之一造成永久傷害的方式。

1. **D** contain v. 包含。(A)改為 is composed of　(B)改為 consists of　(C)改為 is made up of

2. **D** have effect on... 對…有影響。

3. **A** need to + V 需要做…。(C) need + V-ing 需要被…，語意錯誤

4. **B** 維持大氣平衡與防止全球暖化 (global warming) 為因果關係，故選表原因、方法的 by。

5. **B** 前半句提到雨林的價值不能以金錢觀點衡量，而本格後表示這卻是實際上現行的方式，根據語意填 unfortunately (不幸地)。(A)幸運地　(C)(D)因此

6. **A** A be replaced with B = B replace A A 由 B 所取代。(B) A substitute for B 以 A 代替 B，不能用被動式。(C) 由…所供應　(D)被…所改變

7. **C** be used to + V 被使用來做…。句意為「…被用來製造橡膠和紙張」。

8. **C** 後半句提到的土壤 (soil) 受損情況，是在前半句雨林被破壞的情形下才會發生的，故選 once (一旦)。(A)…之前　(B)直到…　(D)雖然

9. **A** 用現在進行式表示「雨林正在被破壞」這個令人擔憂的事實。

10. **D** expect sb. to + V 期盼某人做…。take advantage of 利用。leave... alone 不管，不打擾。根據句意與文法選擇(D)。

Unit 17
線上購物——便利又趣味

　　在今日的繁忙世界，購物者講求便利性。這是近來全球出現網購榮景、電子商務獲利豐厚的原因之一。現在只要在行動裝置上簡單按個鍵，就能上網買到流行的法國洋裝、訂飛往東京的機票、或向在地餐館訂披薩。

　　三項新近調查顯示，儘管親臨賣場仍是最常見的購物方式，但全球各地有越來越多消費者上網購物。也有更多消費者進行全球採買，向海外商家下訂單，並更快收到貨。

　　一項調查指出，逾60% 的臺灣網路用戶上網買東西，每人每年平均消費新臺幣 16,586 元。16% 的臺灣網路用戶也上網賣東西。在台灣消費者之間，最常網購的是衣服、旅遊行程和旅館住宿預訂、機票、活動門票，以及日用雜貨。臺灣消費者說，上網買東西是因為他們喜歡其便利性，再

加上購物結帳前可查閱產品評價。

　　雖然顧客重視便利性，但大部分人沒撿到便宜不肯花錢。消費者想要天時地利、價錢合意時才買。網路提供種類繁多的產品和服務，供消費者比較。最棒之處在於，通往這家虛擬商店的大門永遠不打烊！消費者可以享受隨時隨地採買的便利性。

1. **D** 此處表示「…的原因」，而且在空格後面是完整的句子，故空格內的答案可以是 that 或 why，在選項只有 (D)符合要求，故為正確答案。如果在空格後面是名詞片語，則空格內必須使用 for。

2. **C** 此處的 with 意指「使用…工具或方式」的意思。見 **Unit 10 Extension**。

3. **B** 空格前後都是完整的子句，前一句是「三項最近的調查指出，全世界有愈來愈多的人正在進行網路購物」，而後一句是「親自到店裡選購仍然是最受歡迎的購物方式」，兩句的句意明顯有對比，因此可以得知應為副詞子句中的「讓步子句」，故選擇 although 這個連接詞。見 **Unit 17 Extension**。

4. **D** 由於選項中都沒有包含連接詞，因此可以判斷此處為分詞構句的句型。而主要子句的主詞是 more consumers，兩個動詞分別為 order 和 receive，依句意判斷，必須使用主動式的分詞構句，故應變化為 ordering 和 receiving。

5. **A** 本句的意思是「…，每個人每年平均花費新臺幣 16,586 元」。(B)範圍，程度 (C)印象 (D)產出，生產

6. **C** 本句主詞是 "the most popular online purchases"，為複數名詞，而且依後一句來判斷，時態為現在式，

故要選擇 are。

7. **C** 此處為關係子句簡化所形成的分詞片語，用來修飾 the convenience，原句為 "...they like the convenience which is combined with the ability to..."，把關係子句內的主詞和 be 動詞省略後，留下過去分詞 combined 來修飾原本的先行詞。

8. **A** 因為空格前面是介系詞 without，因此本格要選擇 getting。

9. **B** 本句的意思是「網路提供了範圍廣泛的產品與服務讓消費者去比較」。(A)適應 (C)刪去，省略 (D)渴望

10. **D** 本句的意思是「最棒的是，這間虛擬商店的門是全天候開放的！」(A)偶爾 (B)從遠處 (C)遲早，早晚

Unit 18
維他命

　　維他命的研究可能是醫學研究中成長最為快速的領域。儘管一般大眾似乎相信維他命的功效就跟製造廠商說的一樣，並且一窩蜂跑去購買維他命，但維他命到底是什麼，而消費者又應怎麼使用，其中仍有不少的誤解與迷思，而研究結果已經證明這些迷思都是錯的。

　　首先，許多維他命根本達不到宣稱的功效，從未有證據顯示維他命 C 能有助於預防感冒，維他命 B 群也無法消除疲勞，舉例來說，覺得服用維他命 B-12 有效，不過是心理作用罷了。B-12 缺乏症非常少見，就算是需要維他命 B-12 治療的病例，也是用注射的方式，因為口服的效果不彰。

　　一般人常說維他命 E 能預防心臟疾病，增強生殖能力，並延緩老化，但公鼠攝取維他命 E 不足會造成不孕，並不代表人類有相同問題時也會發生同樣的事情。

最常見的維他命是 A、B-1、B-2、C 和 D，而且你只要有能提供這些維他命的均衡飲食，就沒必要再服用任何額外的維他命丸。縱然有許多人認為你應該吃些特殊的食物或每天服用維他命丸，以確保能攝取適當的維他命量，但這根本不對。其實，這麼做的話你很可能補充過量的維他命，有些維他命若攝取過量會產生毒性。事實上，比起維他命缺乏症，服用過量的維他命常會造成更嚴重的後果。而且，這種情形也日益普遍。

1. **D** despite *prep.* 儘管。
   (A)幸虧 (B)因為 (C)改為 In spite of
2. **D** 本句可還原成 ...many vitamins will not do the thing which is often claimed (宣稱)，故填 what。見 **Unit 15 Extension**。
3. **A** get rid of... 免除…。
   (B)放棄 (C)相處 (D)忍受
4. **B** 後半句舉例來說明前半句，故用 for example (例如)。(A)結果 (C)總而言之 (D) (理由) 一則為
5. **C** orally *adv.* 口服地。本句為分詞構句，因語意被動，故選 taken。詳見 **Unit 18 Extension**。
6. **A** 延緩老化過程。
   (B)接近 (C)節目 (D)計畫
7. **B** sth. happen to sb. 某事發生在某人身上。(A)屬於 (C)談到 (D)與…比較
8. **C** 「一個人若有能提供這些維他命的均衡飲食…」。(A)保護 (B)防止 (D)應改為 consist of (含有)
9. **C** in fact 事實上。(A)應改為 Actually (B)也就是說… (D)總而言之
10. **D** 相較於維他命不足 (deficiency) 的是過量用藥 (overdose)。

Unit 19
愛滋病知多少

愛滋病正在全球蔓延，是一種會摧毀人體免疫系統，在生物學上很複雜的疾病。每天約一萬六千人感染人類免疫缺乏病毒 (HIV)，最後會轉變成愛滋病。由於愛滋病還無法治癒，得病的人最終難免一死。因此，讓大家更了解這個疾病就格外重要。如此一來，大家知道如何採取正確的預防措施，愛滋病的散播將可望得到控制。

愛滋病的病毒是由人的血液所傳染的，一個人接觸到另一個人的血液時，就有可能接觸到愛滋病病毒。愛滋病傳播途徑主要有三種，最常見的方式就是和已經染病的人有性接觸。未採保護措施的性行為十分危險，因為和另一個人發生性行為，不是只有和這個人接觸，而是等於和其性伴侶有過性行為的所有人接觸。只要愛滋病侵入一個群體，就會快速傳給更多其他的人。

因吸毒或是其他目的而使用針頭，也有染病的風險。吸毒者與別人共用針頭，就和別人的血液有了直接的接觸，如果其中有人有愛滋病，那另一個人就有可能得到愛滋病。第三種感染愛滋病的途徑是經由輸血。假設有人發生意外而需要輸血，他或她接受的血液有可能帶有愛滋病病毒。目前這種感染愛滋病的途徑很少見，不過在較為貧窮的國家，這仍然是一項危險因子。由於幾乎沒有捐血者接受愛滋病檢測，接受血液者仍舊處於危險。

1. **B** contract *v.* 染患 (疾病)。本格引導的非限定關係子句，修飾先行詞 HIV，必須填 which。(A) who 用於先行詞是人時 (D) that 不用於非限定關係子句
2. **C** 治療法 (cure) 後慣用介系詞 for，表

示「治癒…疾病的療法」。

3. **A** in this way 如此一來。

(B)絕不 (C)順便一提 (D)在途中

4. **A** 先行詞為 ways (方法)，需填 how 或 in which。見 **Unit 19 Extension**。

5. **D** 本句後面談到未採取保護措施的性行為十分危險，可知本句所指的傳染途徑是經由性接觸。

6. **B** once *conj.* 一旦。

(A)雖然 (C)直到 (D)除非

7. **C** risk + V-ing 有…的風險。(D)接觸

8. **A** in contact with... 和…接觸。

(B)和…比較 (C)回報… (D)關於…

9. **D** 本句描述發生意外而需要輸血的人，故選(D) receive (接受)。

(A)捐贈 (B)歸還 (C)去除

10. **D** 前句提及目前這種感染方式很少見 (rare)，而本句卻語氣一轉，表示在較貧窮的國家它仍然是項危險因子，故填 however (然而)。

(B)換句話說 (C)因此

Unit 20
圖像文學

藝術和文學的關係可回溯至數千年前。在印刷品廣泛可得之前，故事都靠口耳相傳。繪畫也是極富價值的敘事形式，有助神話和傳說流傳千年。時至今日，從雜誌詩作、兒童小說到成人漫畫等多種文學形式，插圖都扮演重要角色。

兒童繪本提供了內文和插圖如何緊密連結的範例。兒童心理學家已指出，圖畫對學習閱讀的小孩很重要。事實上，即使是沒有文字的圖畫書，都能藉著發展「自己讀」的概念，幫助幼童閱讀。對成人來說，圖像文學以漫畫書的形式逐漸走紅。這些漫畫本來主攻青少年讀者，現在卻有

許多成人也在看。漫畫探究的主題橫跨輕鬆談笑和深奧哲學。童書和漫畫裡的插圖逐漸獲得認可，被看作視覺藝術的一種嚴肅形式，和繪畫與雕塑等傳統形式一樣受到推崇。出版業現已有一些聲譽崇隆的國際獎項，頒給最佳插畫家。

隨著藝術家和作家探究插圖和文學作品之間的各種可能性，兩者的結合持續進化。數位革命讓插畫家和作家擁有新自由，可攜手合作發揮創意。未來會有更多有圖像文學提供給線上讀者，或以傳統書本形式呈現。

1. **C** 本句的意思是「…故事是用口述方式而被傳遞下去的」。

(A)過世 (B)經過，路過 (D)昏過去

2. **B** 本句的意思是「他們也有助於使神話與傳說長久地存活流傳下去」，其中的 keep...alive 是指「使…活著或存留下來」。

(A)睡著的 (C)獨自的 (D)清醒的

3. **B** play a(n) adj. role/part in... 在…當中扮演了一個…的角色。在此片語中，動詞 play 為固定用法，不能更改，故選(B)。

4. **A** 由句型結構來判斷，可以得知此處空格後面是一個名詞子句，當作介系詞 of 的受詞。此外，由於空格後面為完整的子句，故可判斷空格內只能使用 how。

5. **D** 由於空格在介系詞 by 的後面，故要選擇動名詞 developing，而此處的 by 是指「藉由…的方式」。

6. **A** 本句意思是「這些漫畫書過去曾經主要是給青少年看的，但是現在許多成年人也在看這些漫畫書」，此處 used to + V 是指「過去曾經」。見 **Unit 20 Extension**。

7. **C** range from...to... 範圍從…到…。

8. **D** as adj./adv....as... 像…一樣地…。

9. **D** a number of + 可數名詞指「一些…」，而 the number of + N 是指「…的數目」，至於 an amount of 雖然也是指「一些…」，但後面要接不可數名詞。

10. **B** 本句的意思是「插圖和文學之間的結合持續演變…」。
    (A)盤旋，停留在空中 (C)在商店裡順手牽羊 (D)急速下降

文意選填

Unit 1
鹽商與驢子

有一天，有個經營鹽業的商人趕著他的驢子到海邊去買鹽，回家的路上橫越一條小溪，就在過溪的時候，他的驢子失足意外地跌進水裡，驢子重新站起來以後，身上的負擔變輕許多，因為水把鹽溶化了。商人折返回去海邊，把比先前更多的鹽裝載在驢子身上，之後又來到小溪時，驢子故意在同一個地方跌倒，站起來之後，背負的重量又大幅減少。商人看穿了牠的伎倆，就把驢子第三度趕回海邊，這次他不買鹽了，反而買了一整簍的海綿。到達溪邊時，驢子又打算故技重施，牠再次故意跌倒，結果海綿因為水分而膨脹，牠的負荷大為增加，背上的負擔因此而加倍，牠得到應得的懲罰了。

1. **E** 由 across 可知，前面動詞應為不及物動詞，lay 是 lie (位於) 的過去式，為不及物動詞，故填 lay。「他回家的路上橫越一條小溪」。

2. **D** 由 made a false step (失足)，得知驢子是意外地落水。

3. **F** 驢子的負擔 (load) 變得較輕，是因為水溶化了鹽。

4. **G** a large quantity of... 大量的…。此處用 larger 表「更大量」的鹽。

5. **A** 由後兩句「商人看穿了 (see through) 牠的詭計…」，可知這次驢子是故意地跌倒。

6. **H** with 引導介詞片語，結構為 with + O + OC，表示伴隨主要子句而來的情況。對照第四句，可知驢子負擔的重量在跌進小溪後被減少了。

7. **I** 由第一句及第五句，可知這是商人

第三次 (for the third time) 去海邊。

8. **C** 由「一簍海綿 (a cargo of sponges)，而非是鹽」可以知道是本句提到商人購買的貨物，故用 bought。

9. **J** play a trick 耍詭計。

10. **B** 由本格後「給牠的背加倍的 (doubled) 負擔」，可知牠的重擔大大地被增加了。

Unit 2
避免短路之道

我們很多人在生命中某個時刻會面臨「短路」。然而，若你在陷入危機前採取行動，這是可以預防的。

首先，你必須決定在你生命中什麼是真正重要的，並且調配時間給那些對你最有意義的人們和活動。

第二，你需要和他人分享你的感覺。不僅表達喜悅和成就，也要表達你的挫折感，失望和痛苦的經驗。如果你沒有經常這樣做，你會「爆炸」。和他人培養健全的關係會使你堅強，並且帶給你的生活較佳的平衡。

第三，確定你有休假時間，不管你覺得需要與否，要小歇片刻，也要定期休假。學習如何說「不」以便讓你能對那些對你真正重要的事說「好」。找尋活動來充實並提升你的精神層次，例如音樂、舞蹈、運動、按摩或冥想。並且安排一些自己獨處的時間。

最後，如果你需要幫助而且所有其他的方法都無效時，尋求合適的醫生吧。這一點也不可恥。更重要的是，這也許正是恢復你的精神健康所需要的。

1. **G** 本句指出前句的情況是可以預防的，用 however (然而) 表語氣轉折。

2. **E** meaningful *adj.* 有意義的，呼應本

句前半部的 really important (真正重要的)。

3. **C** 下一句建議讀者表達 (express) 自己的各種情感，因此可推知此處為「與他人分享你的感覺」。share sth. with sb. 和某人分享某事 (物)。

4. **J** A as well as B 不僅 B 而且 A。不僅表達正面的喜悅、成就，也要表達負面的挫折、失望和痛苦的經驗。frustration *n.* 挫折。

5. **B** balance *n.* 平衡。由本句的主詞 Nurturing healthy relationships... (培養健全的關係…)，推知此處選一正面意義的名詞，而非(H) shame。

6. **I** 用 and 連接前後對等的名詞。與 short breaks (短暫的休息) 對等的是 regular vacations (定期的休假)。

7. **F** so that... 以便…。

8. **A** 本格後面列舉可充實及提升精神層次的活動，故用 such as... (例如…)。

9. **D** 當前述方法皆不奏效時，必須尋求合適的醫生。

10. **H** shame *n.* 羞恥。尋求醫生幫助這件事「一點也不可恥。更重要的是，它也許正是恢復你的精神健康所需要的」。restore *v.* 恢復。

Unit 3
鼓勵

但丁‧蓋伯‧羅塞提 (Dante Gabriel Rossetti) 是十九世紀著名的詩人及畫家。曾經有位長者前去找他，這名老人有些圖畫想請羅塞提過目，然後再跟他說這些畫作是否有什麼優點。

羅塞提仔細端詳，看過前面幾張後，他就知道這些畫毫無價值，連一丁點的藝術天份也沒有，不過羅塞提是個好人，他

盡可能委婉地將真相告訴老人。他說這些畫沒有什麼價值，也顯現不出什麼才能。他很抱歉，不過他不能向這個人說謊。

這名訪客很失望，不過他似乎已經預期到羅塞提的評價了，接著他為了占用羅塞提的時間而道歉，但懇請他能否再多看幾幅畫，幾幅由一位年輕美術學生所作的畫。

羅塞提看了看這些畫作，馬上為這些作品展現的才能感到興奮，他說：「這些…，這些很不錯。這位年輕學生很有天份，在他往後成為藝術家的生涯中，應給予他所有的幫助與鼓勵。他的前途不可限量，只要他能埋頭苦幹，堅持下去。」

羅塞提可以感覺到這名老人深深受到感動，他問道：「這位年輕有為的藝術家是誰啊？你的兒子嗎？」

「不是，」老人難過地表示：「是我，是四十年前的我。要是當時能聽到你的讚美就好了！如同你看到的，我受到了挫折，而且放棄得太早。」

1. **E** have a look at... 看一眼…。

2. **I** as...as possible 儘可能地…。

3. **H** 前兩句提到這些畫「並沒顯現一丁點的藝術天份 (showing not the least sign of...)」，可知填 little (極少的，幾乎沒有的)。

4. **J** 前句敘述羅塞提將心中對這些畫不好的評價告訴老人，可知他雖然覺得遺憾，卻不能向老人說謊。

5. **A** apologize for + N/V-ing 為…道歉。本格後接受詞 Rossetti's time，可知需填動名詞。take up... 占去 (時間等)。

6. **G** 由本段第一句得知，羅塞提對這些畫作所展現的天分感到興奮，因此這個年輕學生必定有極佳的天分。

7. **D** 本格後「作為一個畫家」是指職業

8. **C** 「…老人深深地被感動」。

9. **F** 一段時間 + ago 一段時間之前。

10. **B** If only... 要是…，後接假設語氣，表示強烈的願望或遺憾。老人表示要是當時聽到羅塞提的讚美，就不會如後句所言，太早放棄了。

Unit 4
蝙蝠

蝙蝠邪惡的名聲是容易理解的。這些生物因為攻擊人類及傳播傳染性疾病而被人責難。他們白晝睡眠夜間飛行的事實也增添他們的神祕性。然而，蝙蝠並不攻擊人類，事實上，每年遭受寵物狗及蜜蜂的攻擊而死亡的人數超過遭蝙蝠攻擊而死亡的人數。

蝙蝠在世界各地扮演一項重要的生態功能。牠們每年吃掉數百萬的有害昆蟲。事實上，一隻蝙蝠每晚所吃的食物高達牠體重的四分之一。科學家觀察亞利桑那州的一個蝙蝠群落每晚可吃掉高達三萬五千磅的昆蟲，相當於三十四頭大象的體重！

蝙蝠不久可能將消失在世界上。一則因為牠們正快速失去牠們自然的棲息地，包括洞穴,廢棄的礦坑和某些種類的樹木。蝙蝠也因農夫用以對抗有害昆蟲的化學物質而身處險境。科學家發現單單亞利桑那一州，在過去六年中蝙蝠的數量已由三千萬降至三萬。許多人因不理性的恐懼而殺害蝙蝠。一位蝙蝠專家說:「現今蝙蝠的保育最迫切的需要就是增進大眾的認知和教育。」

1. **D** 蝙蝠「以攻擊人類及傳播傳染性疾病被人責難」。

   infectious *adj.* 傳染性的。

   accuse sb. of... 指控、責難某人…。

2. **A** 「蝙蝠白晝睡眠夜晚飛行的事實，增添 (add to) 牠們的神祕」。

3. **J** 由後句得知，蝙蝠一年吃掉數百萬的害蟲，因此可說其執行一項重要的生態學功能。

   ecological *adj.* 生態學的。

4. **G** 本句用 in fact (事實上)，強調「一隻蝙蝠每晚所吃的食物達到 (amount to) 牠自己體重四分之一」的事實。

5. **H** up to... 高達…。

6. **C** 由前句得知，一群蝙蝠每晚吃三萬五千磅的昆蟲，而磅是重量單位，故用三十四頭大象的體重來與之相比。equivalent *adj.* 同等的。

7. **I** for one thing (理由) 其一為…。由 because 得知此處要陳述「蝙蝠不久將消失在世界上」的原因。

8. **B** destructive *adj.* 有害的。

9. **F** 「…蝙蝠的數量已由三千萬下降至三萬」。

10. **E** 由第一段最後兩句話及第二段判斷，蝙蝠的存在其實是有益處的。因此人類對它的恐懼是不合理的。

Unit 5
肥胖

有太多太多人體重過重，而肥胖或許是現今美國人所遭遇最為嚴重的健康問題，因為它是導致其他多種健康問題的起因。心血管疾病、糖尿病、高血壓、關節炎等疾病，在過重的人身上更為常見。多餘的體重會造成肌肉與關節的問題。許多研究開始將癌症和肥胖連結在一起，因為比起在肌肉中，脂肪組織中更有可能找到癌細胞。

除了自身的健康問題，超重的人可能

在心理上也飽受折磨。過重的人會發覺買衣服成了難事，而相當肥胖的人會覺得飛機的座位和候車室的椅子等公共設施太小。有些肥胖的人表示，他們對於自身的情形感到羞恥，所以會避免外出到公共場合。有些過重的人能不運動就不運動，因為他們過多的體重使運動困難，但隨著活動量的減少，體重更容易增加，因為要是有運動的話，至少能「燃燒」一些卡路里。所以，許多肥胖者陷入運動量少和體重增加的惡性循環中。

1. **E** a contributing cause to... 表示「造成…的原因」。contribute to... 造成⋯。

2. **D** high blood pressure 高血壓。
   diabetes *n.* 糖尿病。

3. **F** link A with B 將 A 與 B 連結起來。由本句後半得知，比起在肌肉中，癌細胞 (cancer cell) 在脂肪組織 (fat tissue) 中更有可能被發現，可知癌症與肥胖有關聯。

4. **C** 上一段提及肥胖的人身體上的健康問題，而本句更提到他們心理上 (mentally) 也受折磨 (suffer)，故填 in addition to... (除了⋯)。

5. **J** 「過重的人發覺他們買衣服很<u>困難</u>」。此處為 find + O + OC 的句型，it 代指不定詞片語 to buy clothes。

6. **G** 「相當肥胖的人發覺像飛機座位和候車室的椅子等公共設施 (public facilities) 太小」。句型同第 5 題。

7. **B** 由本句前半「⋯他們對自身的情形感到羞恥 (humiliated)」，可推知他們「避免外出到<u>公共場合</u>」。
   in public 公開地，公然地。

8. **I** 主詞為 some overweight people，可推知本句後半為「他們過多的 (extra) 體重使運動困難」。

overweight (過重的) 一字由 over 及 weight 組成，即有此意。

9. **H** 「隨著活動減少，體重變得容易<u>增加</u>」。it 是虛主詞，指不定詞片語 to gain weight (增加體重)。

10. **A** at least 至少。「⋯因為運動<u>至少</u>能燃燒掉一些卡路里 (calories)」。

Unit 6
「球王」比利的故事

艾德森・阿蘭提斯・多・納西門托，是全球聞名的球王比利，生於 1940 年 10 月 23 日。他們家住在巴西一個小村莊，家境窮苦。他很小就學習踢足球，把身邊所有能當球的東西都拿來練習，連葡萄柚或一團破布也不放過。

艾德森八歲時，有個踢足球的小孩不明所以的給他「比利」這個綽號。這個名字沒有任何意義，因此艾德森認為是在罵他。外號很快傳開，其他小孩也開始叫「比利」。他不惜打架，以避免被嘲弄，直到被處罰兩天不准到校。但還是甩不掉這個外號，沒多久，連他爸爸媽媽都叫他比利。

比利 11 歲時，教練瓦爾德曼・德・布里托注意到他在踢業餘足球。他持續留意比利，四年後，帶他到聖多斯，受訓成為職業選手。起初，比利的隊友對布里托相中比利很意外。但比利一次又一次證明他的實力。在他的職業生涯裡，比利在 1363 場比賽中進球 1281 次。他四度參加世界盃足球賽，三次奪冠。有一次，奈及利亞內戰停火 48 小時，好讓比利能在首都進行示範賽。自此而後，比利被視為是止戰英雄。

比利在 1974 年退休。此後，比利利用他的資源幫助需要的人，透過足球賽增進國家間的情誼。1994 年，巴西任命他為「體育部長」，讓他能繼續在全球推廣運動。

1. **G** 「他的家庭居住在巴西的一個小村莊，…」。

2. **E** for no reason 沒來由地。

3. **C** 由後兩句艾德森因此和人打架，可推知他本人對此綽號有負面想法，故選 insult (汙辱)。

4. **J** start + V-ing 開始去做…。「…其他孩子也開始叫他『比利』」。

5. **B** stop + V-ing 停止做…。「艾德森會與其他孩子打架來阻止他們嘲笑」。

6. **F** 後句提及 4 年後他被帶去訓練成職業球員，可知此句與後句形成對比，此時他仍是業餘球員。

7. **H** be surprised at 對…感到驚訝。

8. **A** 「他的生涯在 1363 場比賽中得到了 1281 分。」

9. **D** civil war *n.* 內戰。

10. **I** 「…透過足球比賽促進國家間的友誼。」

Unit 7
機器人

　　當你想到機器人，心中想到什麼？你想到謀劃要接管地球的邪惡鐵皮怪物軍隊嗎？或者，也許是被一個發狂的天才創造成擔任守衛或士兵的機器人，或許你想到類似真人的機器人，它們的行動、思考和外貌都很像人類。事實上，諸如此類的機器人和科幻電影的關聯性比和實際生活的關聯性大，在真實的世界裡，機器人是一種會代替人類工作的機器，機器人不是可以自行運作，就是在人類的控制之下工作。

　　舉例來說，在一家汽車工廠中，機器人可組合車體和將車身噴漆。在海底，利用有機器手臂的遙控水下機器能執行難倒潛水夫的工作，機器人太空船可以探索太陽系和傳送有關行星和恆星的資訊回地球。

　　許多機器人都有電腦裝置，有些機器人有照相機、感應器和麥克風的裝備，這些裝備使它們能夠看、感覺、聽，有些機器人甚至可以發出電子語言。

　　這一切並非代表機器人能夠像人類一樣地思考及行動，今日的機器人即使在執行很簡單的工作前都必須被輸入大量資料。換言之，時至今日，現實世界裡的機器人仍無法像在科幻電影或小說中一樣獨立思考。

1. **G** 由本格後的關係子句「它們的行動、思考和外貌都很像人類」，可推測填 man-like (類似真人的)。

2. **C** otherwise *adv.* 若不是那樣的話；否則。句意為機器人做那些「原本必須由人類做的工作」。

3. **D** by oneself 自行地；獨自地。「機器人不是自行地運作就是在人類的控制下運作」。
   either...or... 不是…就是…。

4. **J** for example 舉例來說。本段舉例說明機器人的工作，如在汽車工廠中、海底、以及機器人太空船的工作。

5. **A** 本句開頭指出工作地點在海底 (on the seabed)，可推測這裡修飾 machines 的形容詞為 underwater (水中的)。remote controlled 意指「遙控的」。

6. **I** 句意為機器能「執行 (perform) 難倒潛水夫的工作」。

7. **B** 「機器人太空船…可以傳送有關行星和恆星的資訊回到地球」。

8. **F** and 連接同性質的名詞，由 cameras (照相機) 及 sensors (感應器) 推知本格為電子儀器，且本格後指出這三種儀器分別可讓機器人能夠看、

感覺及聽，可推知填(F)麥克風。

be fitted with... 被安裝…。

9. **E** and 連接詞性相同的字詞，前為動詞 think，故選動詞 behave (行動)。

10. **H** carry out... 執行…。

Unit 8
希望——生命的成功之鑰

　　心理學家發現，希望扮演出奇重要的角色。它在學術成就、忍受困難工作、抵抗惡疾等方面給人帶來巨大的優勢。相反地，失去希望成為一個人可能自殺的重大前兆。

　　堪薩斯大學的史奈德 (Charles R. Snyder) 博士是一名心理學家，他設計了一套量表來評估一個人擁有希望的多寡，他表示：「目前為止我們所做的每項研究都證實，希望是預測結果的有力指標。」

　　史奈德博士指出，在希望量表中得高分的人所經歷的困難和得低分的人一樣多，不過他們已學會用充滿希望的方式來看待它，將挫折視為挑戰，而非失敗。

　　他發現高希望程度的人都有下列幾個特質：

・他們會向朋友尋求如何達成目標的建議。

・他們告訴自己，在自己必須做的事情上一定會成功。

・即使身處困境，他們告訴自己，情況會隨著時間漸漸好轉。

・如果達成某一個目標的希望消失，他們會瞄準另一個目標。

・他們展現一種能力，能將一件棘手的工作分解成具體可行的幾個部分。

　　擁有這些特質，人們較易於在人生中獲得成功。

1. **D** 後面列舉了學術成就、忍受困難的工作及抵抗惡疾，可推測此句句意為「希望給人們帶來優勢的不同面向。」

2. **H** 本句談到失去希望 (the loss of hope)，句意與前句相反，故填 by contrast (相反地)。

3. **G** 本格前為現在完成式子句，故填 so far (直到現在)，表示從過去到現在的一段持續時間。

4. **E** 「他設計了一套量表來評估一個人擁有希望的多寡。」

5. **B** as many...as... 與…一樣多的…。此處在 as many 後加入複數名詞 hard times (艱困時期)，為本格前 had 的受詞，表示「經歷過一樣多的困難」。

6. **A** 由後方列舉的各點，可知此格為高希望程度的人所共有的幾項特質。

7. **I** 疑問詞 how 後面加不定詞片語 to achieve their goal 形成名詞片語作 on 的受詞。

8. **J** 前方的 get 為連綴動詞用法，後面接比較級 better，表「漸漸好轉」。

9. **C** 「如果達成某一個 (one) 目標的希望消失，他們會瞄準另一個目標」。aim for... 以…為目的。

10. **F** break A into B 將 A 分解為 B。「…將一件困難的工作分解為具體可行的幾個部分」。tough *adj.* 困難的。specific *adj.* 具體的。achievable *adj.* 可行的。

Unit 9
世界水資源協會——拯救水資源

　　世界水資源協會是由全球各地的會員所組成的組織。其目的是討論出更好的作法，以節約、保護和管理全球潔淨水資源。

該組織嘗試將這些技術傳授給各國政府、大公司，以及其他能對各國水資源問題作重大決策的有力人士。

　　該組織成功舉辦多場國際會議以解決各國政府之間的用水問題。1995 年設立了一個特定的委員會來訂定世界水資源協會的目標。世界水資源協會於是在 1996 年 6 月正式成立。總部設在法國馬賽。

　　世界水資源協會的重要活動大多是舉辦特殊會議，讓世界各地重要人士和專家學者齊聚一堂。世界水資源協會也嘗試確保每個地方的人都能取得潔淨水，並致力讓貧窮國家有水可用。該組織旗下有許多團體，例如水合作機構，並將會費用在協助減少全球用水問題。

　　節約和保護潔淨水對人類至關重要。各國政府多半已認知此一需求，正主動協助世界水資源協會推展的專案獲致成功。

1. **F** 後面提到探討更好的方法來節約、保護和管理全球水資源，可推知此格說的是世界水資源協會成立的目的。

2. **A** 由前方指示代名詞 these 判斷，此格應填複數名詞，代指前句所提到的節約、保護和管理全球水資源之方法。故選 techniques (技術)。

3. **G** 為了水資源問題舉行了許多會議，可知會議目的是要解決問題。

4. **J** 此格應填形容詞。委員會為了要決定世界水資源協會的目標而設立，可知是個特定的委員會。

5. **C** 此格應填副詞。「世界水資源協會於 1996 年 6 月正式成立。」

6. **B** 後面提到法國的城市馬賽，可推知是該協會的地址。故選 headquarters (總部)。須注意，此為單複數同型的名詞，故後方用單數 be 動詞 is。

7. **I** 「…舉行召集全球重要人士和專家的特別會議。」

8. **E** bring sth. to... 將…帶往 (某處)。

9. **D** 文章首句提到該組織由許多會員組成。此處指支出由會員繳納的會費來協助減少世界的水資源問題。

10. **H** 此格應填形容詞。水資源的節約和保護，對世人來說都是相當重要的。

Unit 10
太魯閣峽谷公路

　　中部橫貫公路於一九六○年竣工，耗費了超過數十億元建造，並造成二百一十二名工人失去生命。他們於建造期間死亡。他們的犧牲絕不會為人遺忘。

　　中部橫貫公路經過太魯閣峽谷的路段是從陡峭山壁雕鑿出來，有著山脈、彎曲的隧道這些令人屏息的景色，還有驚心動魄的峽谷景致。

　　行車經過這個路段，要記得的事情就是，這路段雖美，但不過也是一條眾多卡車司機經常用來環臺運輸物品的公路。對卡車司機來說，時間就是金錢。因此，他們從你身邊以危險的高速呼嘯而過時，也毋需驚訝。在欣賞絕佳景色的同時，也要注意自身安全。

1. **C** more than 比…更多。句意為「耗資超過數十億元。」

2. **A** 前方提到 lives，後句提到在建設過程中，可知失去生命的為工人。

3. **I** 由前句「它耗費了…二百一十二名工人的生命。」可知本格填 die (死亡) 的過去式 died。

4. **B** 「他們的犧牲絕不會被遺忘」。sacrifice n. 犧牲。

5. **J** through prep. 通過，穿過。

6. **G** breathtaking adj. 驚人的，令人屏息

的。

7. **H** 不定詞片語 to remember 修飾 the thing，句意為「要記得的事情是…」。

8. **E** 「這段路雖美，它對眾多司機來說不過也是一條公路…」。as 表「雖然」時，可將其引導的副詞子句中的形容詞、副詞等提前：as it is beautiful → beautiful as it is。

9. **F** 「對卡車司機而言，時間就是金錢…」。

10. **D** at full speed 高速地。blow 在本句意指「呼嘯而過」。

Unit 11
急救

　　現今美國主要的死亡原因是心臟病發和意外傷害，當患者等待救護車時，大多數人不是曾在現場，就是未來可能會在現場。如果患者失去脈搏和呼吸，生存的機會將會大幅降低。若在救護車趕到之前，沒人能協助患者維持脈搏和呼吸，則存活率只有 18%。

　　然而，若患者能在第一時間內接受維持生命的急救，則有 98% 的存活機會。隨著開始急救的時間一再往後，機會也越來越渺茫。事實上，失去脈搏四分鐘後，腦部就會開始衰竭；急救若慢了六分鐘，患者的機會則降至 11%。我們每個人都知道在一個人的脈搏和呼吸突然停止時所應採取的措施，是極其重要的。

　　在所有的死因中，有 50% 是由窒息造成。若患者掙扎著要將空氣吸入肺部，要馬上檢查嘴巴或喉嚨中的阻塞物，有時，喘息聲代表氣管部分阻塞，而患者無法正常呼吸。完全沒有聲響甚至更嚴重。這代表氣管已經完全阻塞，可能很快就會導致

患者死亡。

1. **D** wait for... 等待…。ambulance *n.* 救護車。

2. **E** 「若是患者失去脈搏和呼吸，生存的機會大幅減少」。

3. **H** 「假如直到救護車抵達之前，沒人能協助患者維持脈搏和呼吸，存活率只有 18%」。

4. **C** 前句提及沒人協助患者的情況，而本句談到患者若能在第一時間接受急救的情況，前後語意相對，故填 however (然而)。
vital *adj.* 維持生命所需的。

5. **F** 「隨著急救時間越來越晚，存活機會減少」。

6. **I** 本格後「腦部開始衰竭」進一步說明了本句開頭「失去脈搏四分鐘後」的結果，選 in fact (事實上)。

7. **B** 「若急救慢了六分鐘，患者的機會降至 11%」。fall to 降至…程度。

8. **J** take measures 採取措施。本句以不定詞 to take 修飾 measures，表「必須採取的措施」。

9. **A** of all... 在所有的…之中。「在所有的死因中，有 50% 是由窒息造成的。」

10. **G** even 修飾比較級 more serious，用以加強語氣。

Unit 12
黑暗的時刻

　　「全世界的黑暗不足以熄滅一枝小蠟燭的光亮。」

　　在二次大戰期間，英國小說家塞西爾‧羅伯茨告訴我，他如何在一個慘遭德機轟炸的英國城鎮外一座新豎立的小墓碑上面，發現那句話。然後他如何確信它是

句引文,找尋它的出處卻徒勞無功。還有,後來他如何得知,這句碑文並非引用的文句。他也得知這句話出自一位孤獨的老婦人之手,她的寵物被納粹黨的炸彈炸死。

我始終牢記著這句激勵人心的話,與其說是為了它的詩意和意象,不如說是為了它所包含的真理。我覺得,這真理如此簡單而寓意深遠,以致於適用於任何情境。舉例來說,它能被用在不論是一個偉大國家的最黑暗的時刻,還是我們大家都會遭遇到的個人的微小失意。

在沮喪和失敗的時刻,甚至在絕望的時刻,總會有某些事物可以依附。通常都是些微不足道的事——記憶中的笑聲,一個熟睡孩童的面容,風中的樹,事實上是任何能促使我們回想某種深切地感受或摯愛的事物的,都是。任何一個人,不論如何貧困,都會有許多這種小蠟燭。當它們被點燃起來的時候,黑暗便告消逝。

1. **F** 此處說的是他從一塊墓碑上找到前一段文字。

2. **I** 本句敘述他找不到這段引文的來源。in vain 徒勞無功地。quotation *n.* 引用的文字。

3. **G** 前一句敘述他沒有找到它的來源,而本句說他得知了它的出處,依句意推知填 finally (終於)。

4. **A** 用關係代名詞所有格 whose 引導的關係子句修飾先行詞 lady。

5. **J** 由第一句文意及本段的敘述可判斷,這是一句激勵人心的話。

6. **H** not so much A as B 與其說是 A 不如說是 B。

7. **B** so...that... 如此…以致於… 。「這真理如此簡單又寓意深遠…以致於它適用於 (apply to) 任何情境…」。

8. **D** or 連接相對的詞語,句意為其包含

的真理「不論在國家最黑暗的時刻或是個人的黯淡時分」皆適用。

9. **E** 本格之前的 discouragement 和 defeat 都是負面的情緒,even (甚至) 之後須填一個程度更強烈的負面名詞,故選 despair (絕望)。

10. **C** 和空格前的 deeply felt 相稱,必須填一個副詞修飾 loved,故選 dearly (深切地)。

Unit 13
真正的高貴

在平靜的海面上,人人皆為領航員。

但是如果只有陽光而沒有陰影,只有歡樂而沒有痛苦,那就全然不是人生。就拿所有最幸福的人來說吧——他們的人生是糾結的紗線。悲慟和幸福,輪番而至,讓我們悲喜交替。甚至連死亡本身都讓人生更為可愛。人們在生命的嚴肅時刻,在悲傷與失去的陰影下,最接近真實的自我。

在生活和事業的各種事務中,才智的效力遠不如性格,頭腦遠不如心性,天分遠不如由判斷力所約束的自制、耐心與紀律。

我始終認為,如果一個人的內在生活開始過得較嚴肅,外在生活就會開始過得較簡樸。在一個奢侈浪費的時代,但願我能讓世人了解:人類真正的需求是多麼稀少。

後悔自己的過錯,到不重蹈覆徹的程度才是真正的悔悟。比別人優秀並無任何高貴之處,真正的高貴在於超越從前的自我。

1. **B** not...at all 一點兒也不…。

2. **E** take...for example 以…為例。

3. **F** 悲慟 (sorrows) 和幸福 (blessings) 輪番而至 (one following another),

使我們隨之悲傷和喜悅，故選 by turns (輪流地)。

4. **I** 從下一句知道作者對生命的黑暗面有正面的看法，所以本句應該是陳述死亡的正面意義，「甚至連死亡本身都讓人生更為<u>可愛</u>」。

5. **J** under the shadow of... 在…的陰影下

6. **G** and 連接同性質的名詞，故選 discipline (紀律)。regulate v. 規範，約束。judgment n. 判斷力。

7. **A** 在本句中，關係子句 who has begun...within 與動詞片語 begins to...without 結構對稱，可知應填和 simply (簡樸地) 對應的副詞 seriously (嚴肅地)。

8. **H** how + adj./adv. + 主詞 + be 動詞 多麼…。在奢侈浪費的時代，作者但願能讓世人了解人類真正的需要多麼<u>稀少</u>。wants 為可數複數名詞，故填 few。extravagance n. 奢侈。

9. **D** 由 regret (後悔) 判斷答案為 errors，「後悔自己的<u>過錯</u>…」。

10. **C** 修飾不定代名詞 something、anything、nothing 等的形容詞必須置於其後。本句與下句句意連貫，「比別人優秀並無任何<u>高貴</u>之處。真正的<u>高貴</u>在於…」。由後句的 nobility 推知應填 noble (高貴的)。

Unit 14
一個更好的明天

「我只有一盞明燈引領著我的腳步，那就是經驗。」 ——派屈克·亨利

許多人常常感覺奇怪，為什麼歷史家要那樣不辭辛勞，來保存許許多多過去的書籍、文件、和記載呢？我們為什麼要有圖書館呢?這些舊文件和史書有什麼用呢?

因為，有時經驗之聲能促使我們停住腳步、觀察、和傾聽。也因為，有時候經驗正確解讀的過去記載，可以給我們告誡，警惕我們哪些事該做，哪些事不該做。

如果我們想要創造持久的和平，我們必須從人類的經驗中去探求其淵源。舉例來說，從勇敢和熱誠的人們之記載中，我們得到了激勵。在基督教殉道者們的故事當中，歷史記錄著人類的苦難和英勇事蹟。在我們的迷惘及對和平的渴望之中，這些記載一定會有所裨助。

歷史的至高目的是一個更好的世界。歷史對鼓勵戰爭的人們給予警示。歷史對尋求和平的人們加以鼓勵。總而言之，歷史促使我們學習。昨日的記載可以使我們避免重犯昨日的錯誤。並且從歷史當中，我們看見人類的進步。

1. **H** wonder 後接 why 引導的疑問詞子句，表示「對為什麼…感到疑惑」。

2. **B** what good...? …有什麼好處？good n. 好處。

3. **I** 本句將經驗之聲 (voice of experience) 比喻為平交道，能使我們停、看、<u>聽</u>。

4. **E** 「哪些事情該做，哪些事情不該做」是一種告誡。warning n. 告誡；警告。

5. **C** lasting peace 持久的和平。

6. **F** from records 從記錄中。

7. **A** 「在我們的困惑及對和平的渴望之中，這些記載一定能<u>幫助</u>我們」。

8. **D** 下兩句談到歷史對促進 (promote) 戰爭的人給予警示，帶給尋求和平的人激勵 (inspirations)，可知「一個更好的世界是歷史的至高<u>目的</u>」。

9. **J** 前兩句皆談到歷史的作用，本句歸納前述兩句，故填 in short (總而言

10. **G** keep sb. from + V-ing 避免某人做。

Unit 15
我們是在旅途中

不論你在何處，不論你是何人，在此時此刻，以及在我們一生當中的每時每刻，你和我有一點是完全相同的：我們不是靜止的，我們在旅途之中。我們的生活是朝著一個看不見的目標前進的一項行動、一個趨勢、一項穩定不間斷的進展。我們每天都獲得一些東西，或失去一些東西。即使在我們的地位和個性似乎保持絲毫不變的時候，它們也是變化著，因為單單時間的進展就是一種改變。一片荒野在一月就和在七月不同，季節造成了差別。兒童被視為天真的一些行為，如果表現在成人的身上就是幼稚，是年齡區分了他們。

我們所做的每件事情都是朝著某個方向邁進的一步。甚至未做某件事情，這件事實本身也是一項行為。它使我們前進或後退。磁針陰極的作用，是和陽極的作用同樣實際的。拒絕與接受是相同的——它是兩者中的另一個選擇。

你今天是否比昨天更為接近你的港口呢？是的，你一定會更為接近某一個港口一些的；因為自從你的船第一次在人生之海中下水的時候起，你從來不曾靜止片刻；這個海洋太深了，縱然你想尋找一個停泊之所，也不可得；在未駛進港口之前，你是不能停頓的。

1. **D** 由其後的 we are on a journey 及下一句 Our life is a movement (行動)...，推知此處為「我們不是靜止的」。at rest 靜止的。

2. **H** or 為對等連接詞，連接相對的字詞，和 gaining (獲得) 相對的是 losing (失去)。

3. **G** Even when 連接讓步句，「即使在我們的地位和個性似乎保持絲毫不變 (the same) 的時候…」，和 the same 相對的是 (G)，「…它們也是在變化著。」

4. **J** 前句談到一月和七月的荒田不同，可以歸納出是季節不同所形成的差異。bare 原意為「赤裸的」，在此處指田地「光禿禿的」。

5. **A** 大人若有和小孩一樣的行為，則非天真 (childlike)，而是幼稚。

6. **I** one + 單數名詞 + or another = some + 單數名詞 + or other 某一…。one direction or another 指「某個方向」。

7. **B** 同第 2 題以 or 連接，和 forward (向前) 相對的是 backward (向後)。

8. **E** 與 negative pole (負極) 相對的是 positive pole (正極)。「磁針負極的作用和正極的作用是同樣實際的」。magnetic *adj.* 磁性的。

9. **F** 與 accept (接受) 相對的是 decline (拒絕)。

10. **C** 與第 6 題同為表示「某一…」的句型。亦可寫做 one port or another。

20分鐘稱霸 大考英文作文

王靖賢　編著

- 共16回作文練習，涵蓋大考作文3大題型：看圖寫作、主題寫作、信函寫作。根據近年大考趨勢精心出題，題型多元且擬真度高。

- 每回作文練習皆有為考生精選的英文名言佳句，增強考生備考戰力。

- 附方便攜帶的解析本，針對每回作文題目提供寫作架構圖，讓寫作脈絡一目了然，並提供範文、寫作要點、寫作撇步及好用詞彙，一本在手即可增強英文作文能力。